JOAN LOCKE

Loved

Table of Contents

Chapter 1

I have often heard people tell those who are dealing with their deepest struggles, God doesn't give us more than we can handle. I wonder if those who repeat this quote are the same ones who have never struggled a day in their lives. It's just a sympathetic gesture they repeat to give comfort to someone. They don't have a clue what it is to live one day in that person's shoes. These are the same people who lead a calm smooth day-by-day existence. Their lives continue like a tranquil sea, a beautiful calm blue ocean that meets perfectly with the horizon, with no sign of an intrusion of a ripple or sight of an oncoming wave to upset the balance of their perfect world.

As I look back on my life do those who have this privilege of the perfect job, the perfect family, and even the perfect pet, do they truly feel they are the lucky ones, the fortunate ones? Are they stronger than those who have struggled either part or all of their lives? Did God place someone like me in difficult situations to make me stronger? I think living in that perfect bubble only makes you weaker. When out of nowhere disaster strikes and having no previous struggles to build upon and learn how to pull yourself up from the muck. They fall into a deep depression and despair having no previous hardships to build upon and learn how to move on and become a better and stronger person.

My name is Jenna Monroe I grew up in Philadelphia, Pennsylvania. My father left my mother and me when I was two years old. We lived with her mother in a small two-bedroom apartment. I always remember being surrounded by love. My mom did her best as a single parent to be both a father and mother to me. She had a generous heart and always a smile on her face. No one would ever surmise all the hardships she had to endure. She worked long hours in a retail clothing store for minimum wage struggling to make ends meet. We lived with her mother because many times my mom worked nights and weekends and the money, she earned never stretched far enough to pay rent, buy food, pay for a babysitter for me and God forbid one of us had to go to the doctor. She never complained of her simplistic life. When she had a day off on Saturdays, usually twice a month we always went to the movies. I guess this was her escape from such an improvised lifestyle we led. Mom would always take the candy we had left over from home. She explained to me it was better this way. You have your favorite candy to munch on while watching the movie just in case the concession stand ran out. What a better way to watch a film while munching on your favorite snack she always told me.

I knew our lives were to some point limited, but mom always found a way to make me happy. With her discount from her job, she was able to buy me pretty clothes. She knew how important it was for me to always look my very best. She always repeated the same mantra. Study hard and be sure to get a good education so I could have a better life than her. As I grew older, it was probably in middle school that I realized just how poor we were. I would hear my classmates talk about the exciting places they spent their summers and the trendy restaurants their parents took them to eat. I guess because my mom kept me so well dressed no one would guess how poor we really were.

On the very first day of school when our first writing assignment was that infamous essay, "What Was the Most Memorable Event of My Summer Vacation", I wrote a fictitious story about my father, who I never knew, spending most of the summer visiting him and his family in Italy. I would Google famous tourist sites in Rome and Florence that my dad took me to. I would describe each city with such detail that I even believed I was there. Rome with its history-rich, the Coliseum and Florence for its culture, Renaissance art, and architecture and impressive monuments. Not to mention how delicious authentic Italian food was! I don't think any of my classmates questioned my travels since to describe these two cities you surely had to have been there. As part of Public Speaking training we had to read our stories out loud. As I read, I could see my classmates were mesmerized by the exciting details of my summer vacation. The smiles on their faces confirmed to me that they really believed me.

I never sought out a close friendship with any of my female classmates. They live in houses, I lived in a small two-bedroom apartment. I was always afraid if one of my friends came over, they would ask which bedroom was mine so we could hang out looking through magazines and discussing who the cutest boys were in our classes. Little did they know I slept in the same bed with my mom. When I would ask her why she couldn't share the same bed with her mother just like we were doing her answer would always be the same. We should be thankful grandma has let us live with her. This apartment is hers and it was only right to let her have her own bedroom. So as middle school proceeded to high school, I was still very cautious about forming any kind of close bonds.

****

When I turned fifteen, a sophomore in high school. my life forever changed. I remember that day very distinctly. It was a warm, sunny Friday, May afternoon. Not a cloud in the sky. I was looking forward with excitement to going to the movies with mom on Saturday. Mom had her usual Saturday off and we were going to spend the day as usual. As I walked home from school, I approached the apartment building with so much gusto I ran up the outside steps and raced up to the second floor to our apartment. Opening the door with a grin so wide it hurt my face. As I joyfully enter the kitchen, I saw grandma and my mom sitting around our worn-out Formica kitchen table with its three mismatched chairs. One for grandma, one for mom, and one for me.

Grandma sat facing me as I entered. I could only see the back of my mom's head. Grandma was crying uncontrollably, wiping her tears in a paper napkin hunched over the table. Seeing me she abruptly stopped and sat up straight in her chair.

"What's going on?" I asked, frozen with fear.

My mom turned around in her chair. As I got closer to the table grandma got up, kissed the top of my head and told me to sit down as she slowly walked into her bedroom and quietly closed the door.

"Mom, is grandma sick?" I asked hoping her answer would be no.

If my grandma was very sick and died, where would we live, I thought.
Fear took hold of my heart as mom lovingly cupped both of my hands as she answered in a whisper of a voice that is, she who was sick. My heart instantly broke onto pieces.

"Mom," I sobbed, "What's wrong?" "Will we be okay?"

"Jenna, sweetheart," she said, trying to hold back a rush of tears."
"I went to the doctor last week because I was feeling run down and always tired. I thought it was just from working long hours. The doctor ran a few tests and the diagnosis came back that I have pancreatic cancer."

" When will you get better?' I asked hoping what I was hearing was wrong.

I had heard the word cancer before but not the kind she had.

"Jenna, you have to promise me you will stay strong for grandma and also promise me you will finish high school and go on to college."

" Mom, what are you trying to tell me?" Trying to comprehend what she was saying.

"The doctor said I have six months to a year."

"Six months to a year to do what?" I screamed.

"Before I become very sick and die." She said putting her hands to her face to hide her tears unable to say the last word.

As those words tried to make sense to me I yelled that the doctor is wrong, the test results are also. Mom got out of her chair and wrapped her arms around me kissing my cheeks.

"It will be alright," she said somberly, as she walked and began to stare out the kitchen window with her hands folded together against her waist."

I ran into my bedroom and jumped face down on the bed, tears gushing down my face. This bed I shared with her will one day hold only me. I will no longer be able to feel her warm body next to me. As the months dragged on by I prayed she would by some miracle be free of this cancer that was robbing me of the only stability I knew and our lives would go back to being normal again. Grandma suggested I sleep with her so mom could be more comfortable. Every night I went to bed asking God to allow mom to live one more day. I prayed that prayer every single night. The six months never came. Three months later, at the end of August, mom died. My life was over. The most important person in my life was gone forever. Even though grandma tried her very best to comfort and be a mother to me no one would ever be able to replace her.

****

My junior year of high school was filled with tears and depression. I went to bed every night dreaming about my mom and waking up in tear-covered sheets. As usual, grandma did her best to comfort me, but my loss was still too sensitive and great. It was now time to begin applying for colleges. The only two I applied to were Penn State and the University of Pennsylvania. I wanted to be close to grandma so I could go back home and spend the holidays with her.

By the beginning of my senior year, I found out I was accepted to both schools. Mom had left me money from an insurance policy she had taken out while she was working. If I attended Penn State my inheritance would last longer, but I chose the University of Pennsylvania. I did my best to keep my grade point average up and I graduated with honors from high school.

Graduation day was not a happy or joyous occasion for me compared to the excitement my classmates experienced even though grandma was there sitting in the fifth row if the auditorium with a big smile on her face. I knew she was very proud of me. I would have wished it were mom sitting next to her. I know she too would have been proud of me.

It was now the third week of August and time for a freshman to begin orientation. I knew I would miss grandma, but I longed to be living on campus and leaving the sad and hurtful memories of mom behind me.

The first day I arrived I meet my roommate. Her name was Sandy Wells. We clicked from the very beginning and soon for the very first time, I finally considered her my first best friend. My sad dreams of my mom were being replaced with a subconscious smile on my face when I thought about her. It didn't mean I didn't love her any less it was just that those loving memories were being replaced with the happiest moments I spent with her.

Sandy was the complete opposite of me. I was an introvert, always studying and spending most of my days and nights in the library. Sandy, on the other hand, was an extrovert to say the very least. She attended almost every social event the campus offered. It was surprising to me how she did so well in her classes. She would always tell me I was missing out on the best years of my life by keeping my head buried in my books. I needed to get out and have fun. Join some cam-pus social clubs she often told me. Sandy was always trying to hook me up with one of the guys she knew. I dated several classmates here and there. The longest relationship I was in lasted less than a year. I was focused on my studies and this is what I wanted to stay concentrated on. Boyfriends and relationships would come later on. I decided at the end of my sophomore year my major would be English Literature and hopefully go on to graduate school.

It was during senior year that Sandy finally wore me down and I agreed to go with her to one of the last social gatherings on campus.

"Jenna," she said in a desperate tone, please come with me to this last dance on campus."

"We are going to be going our separate ways soon."

"The only way we will be able to keep in touch is either through Face book or Skyping," again begging me to join her.

Reluctantly I agreed to go. I put on a short denim skirt and a tight tank top.

"You sure look sexy as hell!" Sandy said with a big smile on her face.

"I'm sure when you enter the room you will have at least tens guys trying to jump your bones." "I don't think you realize how attractive you are," Sandy replied in a complimentary voice.

As soon as we entered the Student Union, her friends, mostly guys, scooped her up.

"Jenna," she yelled, over the blaring music.

"Text me when you're ready to leave." "I'll go back to the room with you."

"Don't be silly," I yelled back. "I'll let you know when I leave, you stay and have fun."

Feeling like a fish out of water I walked around the hall trying to fit in and not looking so uncomfortable. I walked over the beverage counter and ordered a Diet Coke. Turning to walk away I bumped into the person who was trying to pass me and spilled my soda on his T-shirt.

"I'm so very sorry," I said looking into the eyes of this handsome stranger.

"No problem," he answered, with a sexy smile on his lips.

"I hope you will be able to get the stain out of your shirt? " I answered embarrassed and my cheeks turning red.

"What are you drinking, he asked in a deep sexy voice?"

"It's Diet Coke," I answered sheepishly.

"Well it should be easier to get out than regular Coke since it has no calories," he answered with an infectious grin on his face.

He extended his hand to me and introduced himself. His name was Ethan Steward. He asked me my name and I answered, Jenna Monroe. He told me he was here with his roommate who was nowhere to be found and I told him I was in the same situation.

"Do you attend the university," he asked with interest?

"Yes," I answered. "I'm graduating in May and plan on going to grad school for a Master's Degree in English Literature.

"How about you?" "Are you a student here also?"

He told me he was finishing his PhD. in Computer Programming with an air of pride and accomplishment in his voice. We soon found ourselves inching toward the exit.

"Jenna, would you like to get out of here and take a walk around the campus?"

"Sure, I replied, "that's fine with me." "The music seems to be getting louder and louder." "Let me just text my friend to let her know I'm leaving."

Ethan and I left the campus hall and walked around the grounds. He told me about his dreams and plans for his life and I was in awe of how steady and hopeful he was in fulfilling them. In the back of my mind, I couldn't help but think of the calm blue ocean that meets the horizon with no sign of an interruption of a ripple or an oncoming wave.

As we continued to stroll, he told me his family lives in Chestnut Hill. I knew this was an affluent neighborhood distinguished by its high incomes and private schools. He added both his parents were physicians and he was the youngest of three other male siblings ranging in ages from twenty -seven to thirty- five.

When he asked me about my family, I was almost too embarrassed to let him into my private world. He felt so trusting and sincere, but with an inability to meet his eyes I poured my heart out to him about my life beginning with the fact that I never knew my dad since he left my mom and me when I was two and continued on to my present station in life.

"Are you ashamed of who you are and where you came from?" Ethan asked with concern as his mouth curved with tenderness.

"I have never shared so much of myself with anyone," I answered looking down not able to meet his eyes.

"Always remember your past shapes your future," Ethan responded leaning into me.

We continued walking until we came upon a bench and decided to sit for a bit. Ethan sat gazing with his head tilted upward toward the stars. Without any warning, he asked me if I believed in love at first sight. I told him I really hadn't given it much thought. With no hesitation in his voice, he told me he did and that one day he was going to marry me. Sucking in a quick breath I answered, "You think so!"

Chapter 2

Ethan and I walked me back to my dorm room, our finger intertwined, as he slipped his hand around my waist bringing me close to him. Gathering me in his arms he tilted my chin upward, butterflies fluttered in my stomach, as he placed his warm sensuous lips on mine.

"May I see you again before you leave for the summer?"

"I guess if you plan to marry me you will have to," I answered unable to control my laughter.

Ethan kissed me again, but this time with more passion, lingering, savoring every moment. This is how my new life was beginning to take shape

It was the beginning of April. Ethan and I were inseparable. He rented an apartment two blocks away from campus. Our dates usually started with me meeting him at his apartment with plans to go out for dinner, see a movie, and then return to his apartment, and then eventually back to my dorm. However, as plans often change Ethan and I never left his apartment once I got there. Dinner turned out to ordering take-out, drinking beer or wine, while we cuddled up with each other on his couch watching TV and then into his bedroom where we enjoyed a passionate night of lovemaking.

Ethan kissed me again, but this time with more passion, lingering, savoring every moment. This is how my new life was beginning to take shape.

Ethan was such a wonderful lover. He was gentle and just his smile when he looked at me, all my defenses melted away. His sexy smile and luscious lips sent my pulse racing, longing for his touch. The flames of passion burned inside both of us as we lay next to each other.

One particular night it was rather late and Ethan suggested I stay over, something I had never done before. He promised he would be sure to wake me in time for my first class. When the clock alarm did not go off, I raced out of his apartment. I had missed half of my morning class, but if I hurried, I could make it in time for the second one. Racing to my dorm room I quickly undressed and showered. As I was pulling on my jeans Sandy walked into our room, backpack hanging off her right shoulder.

"Well good morning." "Where have you been?" "I didn't know the library allowed sleep-overs?" she said not able to control her laughter.

"Spill it, who is he?" she asked with excitement.

"Well if you must know," I answered with a quirky smile on my face.

"His name is Ethan Steward." "I met him at the dance you dragged me to," I answered, my cheeks now red from embarrassment.

"Why didn't you tell me about him?" "How long have you been seeing him?"

"A little over a month ago," I answered feeling bad I hadn't told her before.

I quickly started to tell her he was studying for his Ph.D. in Computer Programming and he was the youngest of four male siblings. He grew up in the Chestnut Hill section of Philadelphia. On hearing where he grew up her response was that I had snagged a rich one. When she said that I never considered being lucky because his family was wealthy. For me money was secondary. Having grown up with very little of it, my family was rich in love. I was not attracted to Ethan because of his family's wealth. He was a caring, generous person. He always put himself last, I was his priority and he showed his love and loyalty to me every time we were together. I was fortunate to have found a man who truly loved me as much as I loved him. We were soul mates.

Graduation was quickly approaching. I told my grandma about Ethan and hoped she would be able to attend my graduation and get to meet him. A few days later she confirmed that her neighbor, Mrs. Hudson would be able to take her. I was given four tickets for my graduation guests. One for Ethan, one for grandma, one for Mrs. Hudson, and one leftover. That ticket would have gone to my mom. I knew she would have been so proud of me. Sandy needed an extra ticket, so I gladly gave it away to her.

The big day finally arrived. I was so excited as I stood in front of the full-length mirror in my dorm room admiring myself in my cap and gown. A tear escaped my eye as I thought how proud my mom would be of me. As I exited my room and walked into the crowd filled auditorium my eyes quickly scanned to find familiar faces. When I took my seat, I was able to concentrate more and focus on the audience. My eyes first met his handsome face. His loving eyes were fixed on me with a huge sexy smile on his face. As our eyes met mine a warm glow flowed through me. There was Ethan. Dressed in a navy suit and red tie looking as handsome as ever. As my eyes left Ethan's, I quickly searched for grandma and Mrs. Hudson. A few rows back I could see the two of them talking and laughing

After the ceremony, I was anxious to find Ethan and grandma. Leaving the stage, I hurried to where she was sitting.

"I'm so proud of you, and your mom would be also," she said as she wrapped her arms around me in a loving embrace.

Ethan soon appeared with a beautiful bouquet of lavender roses in his hands.

"Jenna, congratulations babe," "I'm so proud of your accomplishment," as he took me lovingly in his arms and kissed me gently on my lips.

I introduced my grandma and Mrs. Hudson to Ethan. We all stood around talking while the auditorium emptied out. Ethan surprised me by making a reservation for lunch at a nearby restaurant. Unfortunately,
Mrs. Hudson had to get back to care for her husband who was ill. Before they left grandma pulled me aside and told me she loved that and me in the few minutes she spoke with Ethan she could see how much he was in love with me. I kissed her and told her I loved her and would come back home soon for a visit. I told Ethan I had to go back to his apartment to change into clothes for the restaurant. He also needed to go to retrieve something he let in the bedroom. So, the plan was to go back to the apartment, I would change into appropriate clothing and Ethan would get whatever it was that he left behind. Well, as plans often change, once we got home lunch would-be put-on hold. After Ethan came out of the bedroom, I proceeded to unzip my graduation gown. As I let it slip down from around my shoulders onto the floor, I could feel his warm body pressed up behind me as I stood in my bra and panties. Slowly his hands moved downward, skimming either side of my body to my thighs. He picked up a lock of my hair and caressed it gently. Passion pounded the blood through my heart, chest, and head. He slowly led

me to our bed. I pushed him lightly onto his back. As I straddled over him, I started at his forehead and planted tender kisses around his lips and along his jaw. I loosened his tie and began to slowly unbutton his shirt. I could feel his tongue caress my sensitive breasts as his fingers slid under the stapes of my bra and then removed it. Ethan was ten steps ahead of me by now his pants were off and there we lay naked in each other's arms. We took our time to explore, to arouse, and to give each other pleasure as if it was a brand-new experience for both of us.

"Ethan, sweetheart, I think we missed our lunch reservation." I smiled looking at his gorgeous face lying across from me.

"Yeah, you think so, but it was worth it," he replied as he took his index finger and moved a lock of hair that had fallen across my face.

"I'll call the restaurant and see if I can change it to a dinner reservation."

On the way to dinner, Ethan was constantly proclaiming his love for me and how proud he was of me. As we pulled up to the front of the restaurant the valet opened Ethan's door and presented him with a ticket. Ethan came around and opened my door and took my hand as he escorted me inside. The restaurant was simply beautiful. The room décor was very impressive and I thought about what a loving guy he was to want to make this day special for me. Ethan gave his name to the maitre d who in turn asked us to follow him into the dining area. The ambiance of the room was breathtaking. I had never been to a restaurant as elegant as this. We were seated at a quiet, cozy, and corner table away from the rest of the other diners. A waiter promptly appeared with a silver bucket of champagne and carefully poured some into our Chrystal flutes. He left us promising to return soon to take our orders.

Looking across the table a warm glow filled my heart. I was in love with the most wonderful man in the world. How much more fortunate could I get? As we lifted our glasses to toast Ethan told me he was hopefully celebrating two wonderful occasions. When I asked him what he meant he got up from the table, got down on one knee in front of me.

"Jenna, you know how much I love you. " You make me the happiest man in the world." "Will you do me the honor of being my wife?"

Placing his hand into his inside jacket pocket he presented to me a simple, but elegant two-carat pear-shaped diamond engagement ring. With tears rolling down my checks, my hands covering my mouth, shaking my head, yes. Ethan extended his hands toward mine as he placed the ring on the finger of my left hand.

"Jenna, I know we said we would wait to get married after we both finished school, but the truth is I can't wait that long." "I love you so much I was hoping we could get married before school begins."

"Ethan, that only gives us two months."

I could almost see the disappointment in his face as I said those words.

"Babe," I said, "you make me so happy, there's no need to wait. "How about July, I suggested?" still whirling with emotion.

Ethan leaned across the table taking both of my hands placing his firm and sensual lips on the tops of my fingers. I could see by the smile on his face my answer had made him the happiest guy on earth.

Ethan and I planned on a small wedding back home in Philadelphia. It would be small just my grandma and Ethan's family, which I had yet to meet. The following weekend we went to visit Ethan's family so he could introduce me to them. Driving up to his house it was something I had only dreamed of. It resembled a stately Victorian mansion, with four massive white columns at the front of the house. I guess when he saw the expression on my face because he told me not to worry; it's just a house. My family is just regular people; they are going to love you. I asked him how he was so sure of that. His answer was that since he loved me so much they would also. I told him I hoped he was right.

Meeting Ethan's family was a little intimidating, his three brothers, their wives and children, and his parents. It was a lot all at once, but he was right they were just regular people. Ethan's parents welcomed me with open arms and told me that everything Ethan had told them about me he was the lucky one. His brothers liked to tease their little brother and I could tell by the redness in his checks that as much as they taunted him he loved them all. When we left I told

Ethan how lucky he was to have such a wonderful family. Now your part of it he said as his whole face spread into a smile.

July was here already. Even though the wedding was small it made the occasion feel much more intimate. I invited Sandy but she was off in Europe studying and felt bad that she couldn't attend.

We lived in Ethan's apartment and were busy being two full-time students but made a promise to each other when time allowed, we would spend it together doing something special. We usually went to craft fairs or took drives along the Jersey shore. Life couldn't get any better as far as I was concerned.

****

Life has a funny way of changing things around. Late one afternoon just as I was returning from my last class, I saw the red light blinking on the answering machine. The call was from Mrs. Hudson. She asked me to call her as soon as possible. From the sound of her shaky voice, I knew something wasn't right. I quickly returned her call. My instincts were correct. She told me as her voice broke painfully that my grandmother was rushed to the hospital with chest pains and died a few hours ago. As she said those words, I thought I was going to faint. The room started spinning and I had to sit down before I fell down. Mrs. Hudson was kind enough to make the funeral plans since she and grandmas were lifelong friends. She conveyed to me that grandma's wishes were for her funeral to be quiet and simple. All she wanted was her pastor to say a few words and to be buried the next day. I thanked her for taking this responsibility from me. I don't think I could have done it. When I got off the phone it suddenly hit me. I was now totally all alone. I had no family immediate left. It left me feeling numb. When Ethan got home from school, he found me sobbing into my pillow.

"Jenna, sweetheart," what's going on?" "What's wrong?"

Cradling me in his arms I told him about grandma. He told me to rest and he would take care of all the travel arrangements. Luckily, it was a short drive to the funeral parlor. The funeral service was simple as the pastor told about the generosity of my grandmother to the church and the community and that she will be missed and he also thanked Mrs. Hudson for all her help and support during this difficult time for me.

Life continued to go on despite the fact that even though I had Ethan and his family losing not only my mom but also now grandma took a toll on me emotionally. Having spent a portion of my life dealing with heartaches, struggles, and tears I gathered my strength and moved forward.

In January Ethan completed school earning his Ph.D. in Computer Programming and was immediately hired by an International Banking Corporation. The job required a great deal of travel, something Ethan was not happy about since it meant leaving me alone. I still had a few months before I graduated so when he was gone, I kept myself busy with my course work and studies. Ethan and I discussed having a family, two children perhaps, but for now he asked me to put that dream on hold for a few years so I could be with him. I agreed.

I graduated in May. Our lives were moving at a rapid pace. One-night Ethan came home from work with some great news. By the expression on his face, it was something fantastic. When I asked what he was so happy about he took me in his arms and said he was being transferred to Miami and was being promoted as supervisor of his department. It meant a big pay raise and since he was in charge he didn't have to travel as much. He would have six other computer programmers under him. He was so excited and I was excited for him.

Chapter 3

Prior to packing up our apartment in Philadelphia, Ethan and I spent two weeks in Miami house hunting. By the middle of the second week, we finally found a house that would be perfect for the both of us.

It was not far from downtown where Ethan worked. We soon found out the traffic in Miami makes even the closest location a traffic-filled nightmare. It was twenty-five hundred square feet located in east Kendall. The house had four bedrooms, two baths, and a large professional-grade kitchen. The entire floor was Idaho Quartz, natural stone. Two walls were accented with white coral rock and off the family room was a large den. It also included an Olympic –size rectangular pool with an outdoor kitchen and a screened-in patio, great for entertaining.

It was my dream home and to make it picture-perfect a Royal Poinciana tree with gorgeous orange flowers marked to the entrance to our home. I felt that I didn't deserve this wonderful life Ethan provided for me.

Ethan enjoyed his new job and position. One night as we were finishing dinner Ethan asked me if I wouldn't mind having his colleagues and their significant others over to watch football on Sunday. I told him it was fine with me and he didn't have to ask for my permission. With a boyish grin on his face he informed me that the reason he asked was since he was their supervisor, he didn't want his co-workers to bring any food, wine, or snacks. We would host it all. That meant the food preparation was all up to me. I told him it was okay with me since I was home all day it would give me something to focus on. Lasagna or Chili was a good choice I thought for a large crowd. It was no problem. So, as usual, as plans change, this one-time event turned into a weekly happening, something we did every Sunday. Ethan loved getting together with his team and bonding over football.

It seemed to me Ethan's work-related travels were endless since he specifically told me this new position required little to no travel. I was thankful I had the opportunity to travel to exotic places such as China, France, England, and Dubai with him, but after two years I was growing weary and anxious to start a family. I confronted Ethan about my concern and he agreed. It was time to settle down, put family first he said with an irresistible grin as he nestled his face in my neck. We tried and tried to get pregnant but to no avail. I made an appointment for us with my Gynecologist. We both checked out to be fine. The advice my doctor gave us was to relax. It will happen when it happens. I didn't think it was great medical advice but Ethan agreed. I was still young, only twenty-five and time was on my side.

To relieve the boredom of being in the house most of the day and also to get my mind off of trying to get pregnant I decided to join the gym, which was about a mile from my home. It proved

to be a welcome stress reliever and eliminated
some of my anxiety.

****

The house adjacent to us had been empty
since we moved in about two years ago. Returning home from one day I noticed hanging from
the For-Sale sign was now another sigh reading,
Sold.   Since I was home all day, I longed for
someone who would be friendly and I could chit-
chat with occasionally. Two weeks later a moving
van was parked outside the new neighbor's front
door and two cars parked in the driveway. I decided I would give them ample time to get settled
before I welcome them into the neighborhood,
the cull de sac to be exact. Three weeks later I decided today would be the day. I got up early and
baked a fresh key lime pie smothered with a
whipped cream topping. I planned to go over after I returned from the gym. With the pie in my
hand, I walked across to my new neighbor's
house and knocked on the door.

"Who is it?" a voice called from behind the
door.

" It's your new neighbor," I answered.

The door opened.

"Hi, my name is Jenna Steward." "I live
across the way from you."

"I just wanted to say hi, and welcome you
to the neighborhood."

"Please come in.," she answered." My name is Colleen Taylor."

Colleen appeared to be in her early to mid-thirties. She was a very attractive woman. She was tall and had a slender figure. Her long black hair was tied back in a ponytail. We sat in her kitchen talking, drinking coffee and snacking on the pie. Colleen was married with two small boys. Adam her oldest was eleven; he loved sports and participated in every intramural sport in school. Colleen and her husband tried to attend every one of Adam's events if possible. Eric was nine, and the complete opposite of his brother. Eric was seriously into his computer. She added it was sometimes difficult getting him to one of his brother's games because of a lack of a Wi-Fi connection according to him. Her husband Noah was the CEO of a major company based in Colorado and was transferred here. I told her a little about Ethan and myself. After an hour and a half of getting to know my neighbor, Colleen had to leave to pick up her son Eric from school. Colleen thanked me for coming over and said as soon as they got settled, she would love to have us over for a barbecue.

When Ethan got home from work, I told him all about the new neighbors. Keying in on the fact that they were sports-minded, he suggested I invite them over on Sunday for our weekly sports get together with his co-workers. Upon meeting Noah, the following Sunday, I was struck how handsome he was. He seemed to be the same age as his wife and had a wonderful personality. Adam was tall with an athletic build, just as I suspected and Eric was the cutest little boy I had ever seen. He had jet-black curly long hair with bangs that caressed his face. For a young boy, he had inherited the good looks from his dad. I was not sports savvy so I spent most of the time in the kitchen going back and forth making sure everyone had enough to eat and drink. Eric spent his time in the kitchen with me his eyes glued to his computer screen. Sundays at our house became a regular routine for Colleen and her family. She insisted she help me with the food for the next Sunday get together, but I told her it wasn't necessary. I knew she had her hands full with her boys and I appreciated that she offered.

Colleen and I soon became fast friends. One afternoon as I getting the mail Colleen and the boys were getting into her car. Eric was giving her a hard time as usual about going to Adam's game.

"Hey, Colleen," I yelled as I walked up to her driveway.

"HI, Jenna," she replied sounding totally exasperated.

"Colleen, if Eric would rather stay with me, I have no problem watching him until you get back."

"Are you sure about that?" she answered somewhat relieved.

"I'm sure," I replied with a smile on my face.

Eric seemed to be relieved to not have to go.

"We should be home by seven," she said as they got into her car with Adam and they backed out of the driveway.

Ethan was home his usual time. When he spotted Eric on the couch, he sat down next to him. Together they were both consumed in various computer programs. It warmed my heart to see how attentive Ethan was with Eric and I prayed one day soon we would have a family of our own. Eric became a regular fixture in our house eating dinner with us when Colleen was tied up with one of Adam's games. He was always polite and well manned. He thanked me each time for dinner telling me it was the best food he had ever eaten and that he loved me just like he loved his mom. It was these moments that made me again long for a family of my own. When my concerns about not being able to get pregnant would surface Ethan would always comfort me by telling me to relax, let's continue with the fun part of trying to have a baby because once it's here I would probably be too tired for him. I assured Ethan it would never happen. I love him too much to neglect him. I knew he was joking. Each time the pregnancy test proved negative I want into a panic. My biological clock was ticking and I felt as if the alarm would never ring for me.

Chapter 4

Returning home one afternoon from the gym as I pulled into my driveway just about to get out of my car, I heard Colleen yelling at Noah. She was calling him foul names, cursing, and swearing at him and screaming he was a coward and how dare he do this to her. I had never before witnessed this kind of behavior in her. She ran up to Noah and slapped him across his face and then hurried back into the house slamming the front door with a thundering bang. As I peeked into my rearview mirror, I saw Noah get into his car, banging the car door shut and roared out of the driveway. Feeling like I had witnessed an extremely private moment I waited a few minutes before I entered my own house. I waited fifteen minutes before I went over to Colleen's. Approaching her front door, I knocked and called her name. I noticed the front door lock was open. I slowly entered the hallway calling out to her. Colleen was sitting at her kitchen table with her hands pressed to temples and it was obvious from her swollen red eyes something was terribly wrong.

"Colleen, is everything alright?" I asked knowing it was not.

"I was in my car and I heard you and Noah arguing."

"Oh, Jenna." she cried with a sympathetic plea." Noah wants a divorce."

"He said he is no longer in love with me and he left me to tell the boys."

"He's a coward," she said adamantly. "Can you imagine he wants me to tell the boys we're getting a divorce!" He always wants to play the good guy to his sons."

I walked over to Colleen feeling devastated for her as to having received this horrible news and just hugged her as hard as I could.

"Colleen, I'm so sorry." "If there is anything, I can do to help out please don't hesitate to let me know."

Colleen confided in me that things between her and Noah hadn't been great lately, but she thought it was just the adjustment to his new job. She said she never saw this coming in a million years. I could never imagine what I would feel like if Ethan came home and dropped a bombshell like that on me. My heart hurt for my dear friend.

Over the next few weeks, Colleen and the boys were absent from our Sunday get-togethers. I told her it was important for the boys not to interrupt their lives. She just nodded and started crying. Adam was now a senior in high school and Eric a sophomore. She said they were old enough to make their own decisions on what they wanted to do or not do regarding visiting their father. I didn't agree with her, however. I checked on Colleen and the boys every day helping her with her errands and making sure she and the boys had what they needed for school. As the weeks went on Colleen feel deeper and deeper into a depression. I could only think the life she had always lived was in the comfort of that protective bubble of a good life with no interruptions. To help her out I offered to pick up Adam from his sport's activities and sent over dinner to make sure at least the boys were fed. Colleen was becoming severely depressed and it was worrying them. One day Adam came to me and expressed his concerns about his mom's constant sleeping and not wanting to leave her bedroom. As her best friend and out of love for the boys I confronted her about this.

"Colleen, I am worried about you and so are your boys." "I know you have been deeply hurt by the divorce, but you have to try to get your life back on track." "Your boys need you."

" Jenna, I don't think I can get through this." she said as she tried to lift her head from her pillow.

Again, I tried to reason with her that she needed to get back on her feet for Adam and Eric's sake. I promised I would help her any way I could. It took a few weeks more for Colleen to get herself together but she did. She soon went online searching for jobs. Colleen had a degree in business and was able to get a position in a back in downtown Miami as an Assistant Bank Manager. Some days she worked late and I told her I would be glad to feed dinner to the boys. They were old enough to get home from school by themselves and I missed them being present in my house and my life. They had a soothing effect on me when they were here.

Ethan welcomed them to our home. He was loving and sympathetic to their emotional circumstances. Ethan by now had established a special bond with the boys: Adam for his love of sports and Eric for his passion for computers. I guess they were starting to take the place of the family I yearned for but still did not have.

Again, my anxiety of not being able to conceive got the best of me. Ethan and I went back to my doctor and after more tests, he reported the same diagnosis. Relax, when it happens it will happen. I was now thirty-two years old. I wasn't past my childbearing age, but we had been trying for so long I was losing patience and fearing it would never happen. Ethan suggested I get myself involved in something that would help me get my mind off of our situation and try to relax. After giving his suggestion much thought I decided I would like to take a Creative Wring class at the nearby university. Writing had always come naturally to me and I enjoyed it. My plan was to go to the campus and find out when the next class would be open.

****

As Colleen's life started to get back to a more normal track I was happy not only for her but the boys as well. Frowns were now replaced by smiles on her son's faces and I was happy that she was doing well. Colleen's work schedule allowed me to spend time with Eric. Even though he was a junior in high school his house felt very empty to him with his mom at work and Adam a freshman at the University of Colorado. Eric asked me if it was okay for him to come to my house after school to do his homework and wait for his mom. Of course, I said yes to him. Eric had grown up before my very eyes transforming from an adorable nine years old with curly dark hair to a handsome eighteen-year-old young man with a cool medium haircut with short sides. I couldn't help but think of how much he resembled his dad, but to mention that was a sore subject I didn't want to discuss with him. It brought back too many hurtful memories that I knew he tried to put behind him. As Adam got older, he reconciled with his father, but Eric did not. He said he could never forgive his dad for what he put them through.

I knew deep in my heart that even though Eric enjoyed my company he would soon want to spend more time with his friends. Little by little these visits stopped and loneliness started to settle in. He was not my son, but I loved him as if he were.

Chapter 5

Lately, I noticed things with Ethan was changing. He was becoming more and more anxious. I asked him several times what was wrong, but he always told me it was nothing and not to worry about him he was fine. I will never forget this one particular day. Ethan came home a little bit earlier than usual and I could tell by the expression on his face something was seriously wrong. Coming into the kitchen I noticed his shirt was hanging out of his pants and his tie loosened. Totally out of character for the neat freak he was.

"Ethan, sweetheart, what's wrong?" I asked afraid of what his answer would be.

Ethan walked over to the couch, sat down and placed both hands covering his face. I walked over to him and sat down close to him our bodies touching. I couldn't imagine what could possibly be.

"Jenna," he hesitated, "I lost my job." "I've been fired. "The company is downsizing and they're making cuts from the top." "They are going to outsource my job."

I thought I was hearing wrong. What he said went straight to my heart and to the pit of my stomach. I knew this job was his life. He studied hard his whole to prepare himself for his dream. Working hard to get his Ph.D. and sometimes sacrificing us at times to get ahead. I wrapped my arms around him and whispered in his ear that everything would be all right. I assured him that with his expertise and experience it wouldn't be long before he found employment.

I guess wishing doesn't make it so. The longer Ethan was out of work the more distraught and reclusive he became. Our dinners together turned into Ethan eating in front of his computer searching high and low for a job. Our nights of becoming intimate also stopped. I felt as if the computer was his new mistress. He spent hours on it as if a job was going to appear any minute and if he wasn't glued to his screen, he might miss his opportunity. The days and nights became torturous for me. To see the man, I adored and fell in love become an empty shell. I had never seen him in such a deep depression. Every time I tried to make a suggestion for him to seek counseling, he always had an excuse why he didn't have to go.

I turned to Colleen for help and advice. I didn't know how she could help, but I needed someone to talk to, and a shoulder to cry on. I believed it was at this time Colleen felt like the sister I never had. Colleen always found the time to sit down and let me cry my eyes out in her house over a cup of coffee. Many times, when I met her at her front door, I could see she was exhausted from a full day at work, but she would place her arms around my shoulder and lovingly invited me into her kitchen as I voiced my frustration and fears about Eric's state of mind. She never turned me away. She listened to me for hours to go on and on until I was able to clear my mind. She was truly a great friend and I appreciated her help and compassion.

****

Six months had already passed and I was beside myself as what our future held. One afternoon as I prepared lunch, I was about to bring it into the den when Ethan emerged with a smile on his face, something I hadn't seen in months. He had applied for a position, similar to what he was doing, soon after she was terminated. The job was in California. The CEO of the company wanted to interview him and he would travel to California on the company's private jet. My heart skipped a beat as I began to believe there was hope and our lives were going to finally be turned around for the better.

That night was sat down together for dinner for the first time in six months. We also slept in the same bed. As we lay together the second Ethan's hand touch my face, I knew the man I loved and adored was back with me. Hypnotized by his touch, I tingled under his fingertips. An act was sparked by that one indelible kiss. A wave of passion and love flowed between us. I didn't want the night to end.

Ethan's interview was to be in two weeks. For the next fourteen days, our lives seemed to get back to normal. The traces of his life six months prior had vanished. We planned things we wanted to accomplish in order to move forward. Ethan remained apprehensive about everything since the job was not a done deal yet. But I convinced him that once they interviewed and discovered how talented he was the job was his. Someone had to remain hopeful and it would be me. I was selfish in my thoughts as I realized I would be leaving Colleen and her two sons. I had grown especially fond of Eric.

The night before Eric left, he promised he was committed to having a family and he loved me. As we lay in bed tears filled his eyes.

"Babe, I'm so sorry for what I put you through these past months." I love you more than life itself and I promise to make it up to you."

I wiped the tears from his masculine face with my index finger and kissed his lips as I told him I loved him and always will.

Monday morning arrived too soon. I drove Ethan to the small private airport in west Kendall. In the distance was the G550, the corporate jet. I kissed him good-bye and he promised to text me when he landed. I watched as he walked away and boarded the jet. I was anxious
for some reason, but I chalked it up to just being nervous for him.

I returned home with a feeling of despair. To get my mind off of Ethan I decided to set up the front bedroom, which I had planned on using for a nursery for my writing corner. I had leftover lavender paint in the garage and decided that it was the perfect color.
Hours later Ethan texted me that he had landed and I also spoke with him that evening. He

asked me to wish him good luck. I told him he didn't need it because he was so talented, he would be a great asset to their company. I spent a restless and sleepless night worrying about Ethan's interview. It wasn't a done deal yet, but I had every confidence in him he would get the job. Tuesday morning, ten o'clock eastern time, Ethan called with fantastic news. The interview went better than he had expected. The job was his. I was so excited for him, for us. He told me since he was coming home late, he would take an Uber and he would see me tonight. Before he hung up, he told me how much he loved me. A warm glow flowed through me as he said those words. I could never love anyone as much as I loved him. I decided to go to the gym to relieve some of the tension I felt lately. I returned home mid-afternoon sweaty but feeling refreshed. As I was making my way to the shower there was a knock on my door. I opened it without asking and before I stood a female police officer and two gentlemen dressed in expensive black suits.

"Are you Mrs. Jenna Barnett?" the female officer asked.

"Yes, I am'" I answered with fear and anguish knotted inside me.

"Mrs. Barnett, may we come in?" asked one of the dark-suited gentlemen.

"Yes, please do." still questioning why three people were at my front door.

I showed all three into the den and we sat down on the couch.

"Mrs. Barnett," one of the men said. " I'm Philip Preston and this is Bill Wilson and Officer Reed. They both worked for James Wallace the owner Ethan would have worked for.

"I'm sorry to have to tell you, your husband Ethan was killed this morning." "The jet he was on crashed on take-off."

I felt as if my head was spinning out of control. I thought I was going to vomit.

What was he saying?

"This must be a mistake." "Ethan can't be dead.
"We just started to get our lives back to normal. "

My whole body was shaking uncontrollably. I felt a pair of comforting arms around me. It was Colleen holding me tight she heard every sad and traumatizing detail.

She must have seen the vehicle parked outside my house and knew something was wrong.

"Oh, Jenna." "I'm so sorry." "Words can't describe how you must feel." "I want you to know I'm here for you every step of the way."

Colleen's words were a blur, but her being here with me was what I needed. I knew I couldn't deal with this all by myself. I remembered asking one of the gentlemen if it could possibly be a mistake, maybe Ethan survived the crash. With his head tilted downward he slowly brought it back up as he looked at me and said there were several eyewitnesses. They saw Ethan board the jet and then it tried to ascend.

A small memorial service was held in Philadelphia. Ethan's family was present along with and his former co-workers, Colleen, her sons, and ex-husband.

Colleen was my support. If it weren't for her I don't think I would have survived. Despite her commitment to helping me get back on my feet, my life was over.

Chapter 6

It was a rough year, but I was slowly getting back on my feet. Life as I had known it was gone and I had to concentrate on a new life for myself, all alone. Thankfully, I was able to move ahead. I realized I was now responsible for every aspect of my life. I had no one in my life to rely on other than Colleen, but she had her boys and I didn't want to be a burden. I had to try to put my pain in the past and move forward. One of the first activities I resumed was going to the gym. I made sure I was there at least three times a week. Excuses were not tolerated. I also decided to re-enroll in the Creative Writing class I had signed up for the previous year.

The first day of school was exciting, but I feared I had bitten off more than I could handle. I was thirty- three years old in a classroom full of twenty-year-old. Somehow, I don't think I fit in, but I reminded myself I was here to learn, not to make friends. Dr. Martin Johnson was the instructor. He allowed me to audit his class, which meant I was still required to complete all the assignments, but I would not receive a grade. Over the course of time, he not only became my mentor but my friend. Dr. Johnson was in his early sixties, married with two adult children. As we became closer, he told me I reminded him of his daughter. I felt honored that he thought of me in that way. He encouraged me every step of the way to help perfect my writing skills. He gave me the confidence in myself to enter small writing essay contests through the Writer's Digest and Universe Magazine. Although my entrees never won first place for publication, I knew I had found something in my life to keep me moving forward and to begin to live my life alone.

Colleen's life had turned around for her. She began dating her boss, Max Phillips. She was head over heels in love with him and she wanted me to meet him. We made a date to have dinner at her house on a Friday night. The dinner was delicious and we had a wonderful time as we talked and laughed around the dining room table. My first impression of Max was that he was a wonderful man and truly loved Colleen. I was happy for both of them.

The following summer, Eric, now eighteen graduated from high school and was accepted to UCLA for Computer Engineering. I had not seen Eric too often lately. He was busy with his friends and school. Somehow, he had always been a comfort to me and I knew I would miss him. Before he left for California he stopped by. I told him I was proud of him and that anytime he was back home I would love to see him. He kissed me on my cheek before he left and little did, I know it would be four years before I saw him again.

Dr. Johnson spoke to me about writing a short story of about ten thousand words to submit for publication. He had confidence in me that my writing had progressed to the point that I could possibly get a story published. He agreed to work with me to accomplish this goal. My days became very busy with attending class and working on my novel. I was taught to write about what

I knew and build upon my past experiences for my inspiration. Naturally, the only thoughts I had were based on my struggles growing up and my life with Ethan. It was these things that were the premise for my book. I found my thoughts came easily for me as I wrote. Eight weeks later my book was completed. I brought a copy to Dr. Johnson to be edited and reviewed. I returned home the gym early one evening my cell phone rang. The caller ID displayed it was Dr. Johnson.

"Hi, Dr. Johnson." "How are you?" surprised to receive a call from him at home.

"Jenna, I hope I didn't get you at a bad time, but I couldn't wait until tomorrow to let you know I just finished your book." "It's wonderful." "I think you have a real winner here."

I was speechless. I couldn't believe what I just heard.

"I'm so happy you liked it, but where do I go from here?" I asked totally astonished.

"Jenna, be at my office by eleven-thirty to-morrow morning and we can discuss what to do."

I thanked him for all his help and also re-minded him I could not have done it without his help. As I got off the phone, I wished Ethan was here with me. He would have been so proud of my accomplishment. I had to splash cold water on my face to stop the tears that were about to roll down my cheeks. Eleven thirty sharp I en-tered Dr. Johnson's office. He greeted me with a big hug and smile on his face. As we sat in his office, he conveyed to me that I was a natural at writing. Your story was so poignant and sincere. I was totally surprised by his comments. I thought the story was good, but not that good. This was my first novel and I thought it was fair even though I had put my heart and soul into it. Together with over the next few weeks, we worked to finalize my novel for publication. Dr. Johnson knew a colleague who worked for a private publishing company. After he spoke to him, he agreed to read it with no guarantees. It was afoot in the door and I was thankful to have gotten this far. Dr. Johnson mentioned I probably would not hear back for a while. It was during this time I spent many hours refining my writing skills. I enjoyed the new path was life was taking.

Colleen's happiness was spilling over to me. She frequently tried to set me up on blind dates with her male co-workers or friends of Max. I continued to tell her I wasn't ready to date and I held fast to my decision.

Chapter 7

It's funny how fast the time flew by. I am now thirty-eight years old and my life seemed to have taken on a new purpose. Colleen wanted me to travel with her and Max to California to attend Eric's graduation. I thanked her but; I knew when three was a crowd. I sent a card and enclosed a cash gift and reminded her to give him my best wishes and my congratulations.

Dr. Johnson retired from the university, but he still found the time to help me with my writing. The novel I submitted was rejected, but I still had hope, I didn't give up. I rewrote the novel and submitted to another private publishing company. They were willing to publish it. I would receive the royalties from the sale of the book however small the amount would be, but I was still very excited. It was a start for a new author like myself so I sighed on the dotted line. In my contract, I also had to commit myself to signings in four privately owned bookstores spread across the United States. One afternoon while I wrote in my kitchen, sometimes I found it necessary to switch up places to write my doorbell rang. I asked who it was and the voice responded it was Eric. I quickly opened the front door and to my surprise stood a six-foot, three-inch, dark-haired, blue-eyed handsome man. I thought to myself how could he have gotten more handsome from the last time I saw him.

"Oh my God Eric!" "I can't believe it's you." "What are you doing here?" "Does your mother know you're back in Miami?"

"Hello, Mrs. Stewart," he said laughing. "I'm here for a short visit and yes she knows I'm in town." "She's on her way. "I thought I would just stop by to say hello while I wait for her."

I told him to come in and to please call me Jenna. Mrs. Stewart made me feel so old. I led him into the kitchen where we talked for about forty-five minutes until Colleen called to let him know she was home. Eric talked about his new job as a Computer Programmer and how excited he was about starting a new life in Los Angles. I asked him about his upcoming wedding. He seemed hesitant in relating any details. I let it go, I didn't want to pry. He showed my picture of his fiancé and I couldn't help but think she reminds me of myself. Her name was Shelly. She was tall and slender with shoulder-length brown hair curly hair that was parted down the middle. Colleen texted Eric, she was waiting for him and with that, he got up to leave. He added he was also here to visit a few former high school classmates tomorrow and then he would be flying back to LA. I told him I was so happy to have seen him and glad he stopped by. As he stood to leave he walked up to me, placed his hands gently on my shoulders and kissed me on my lips. He told me he loved me and always did. I was shocked by his statement and slightly embarrassed so I told him I loved him also and to enjoy his visit with his mom and friends. Eric's statement or confession to me left me a little unsettled. I really had no idea what he meant by it so I chalked it up to his usual declaration of love for me when he was a young boy. I forced myself back to my writing and soon forgot about it.

I was thankful for my friendship with Colleen. On the weekends we played tennis and spent several afternoons window-shopping in the nearby malls. Colleen shared with me his dreams which included Max. She was hopelessly in love with him and now that the boys were on their own it was time to think of her happiness. She confided in me that Max wanted to get married, but she had reservations about marrying again. She asked for my advice and I told her to follow her heart. Max appeared to be a wonderful and loving man. A month later they were engaged.

My first book was fast becoming a best seller and my contract required me to begin the first of my four-book signings. My first stop was San Diego, and then Denver, on to Dallas, and the last stop New York City. As excited as I was, I was also anxious about it. The travel arrangements were made through my agent, Mark Harris. My only request was for transportation to and from the airports and to the hotel. I also wanted a hotel within walking distance of the bookstore. Mark was in his early forties, a divorced father of two children. He lived in Boston. The few times I spoke with him he seemed to be very nice and easy to work with. The schedule was set and I arrived in my first city Friday afternoon. The signing would be early afternoon on Saturday and a late flight back home on Sunday.

I arrived in San Diego tired but invigorated all at the same time. I checked into my hotel late afternoon and decided to have an early dinner in the hotel restaurant and then retire to my room for the evening. I wanted to be rested and refreshed for tomorrow's big event. I met with the store manager, Will Cutler, an hour before the signing the following afternoon. A table and chair were set up near the rear of the store. On the left side of the table was a stack of my books with a short autobiography about me. It was just like in the movies when I saw the famous author's fans lined up outside the store and around the block, only I wasn't famous and I prayed the line would at least extend to the front door. It was now showtime. I sat at the desk signing my autograph while people expressed how much they enjoyed my book and looked forward to my next one. I was there for over two hours and I would have stayed longer if I needed to. I enjoyed every aspect of meeting my new fans. As I signed the last book I spied a tall male figure in a pair of jeans, a black T-shirt and a corduroy sport jacket. The mysterious figure disappeared behind a row of books at the front of the store. I thanked Will for his kindness and he congratulated me again on the success of my book. As I proceeded to the front of the store the mystery figured appeared. It was from Eric.

"Hi, Jenna." "I guess you're surprised to see me here?" "It looked like you had a good turnout."

"Hi, Eric." "What are you doing here?" "How did you know I was here?" I asked totally surprised.

"I spoke to my mom last week." "She told me you had a book signing in San Diego and I thought it would be great to see you again." He said as he smiled widened as he spoke.

Colleen and I would always keep each other informed of our comings and goings if we planned to be out of town. We usually spoke to each other a few times a week just to keep in touch.

Eric and I left the bookstore and walked around Balboa Park. We stopped for an early dinner at a nearby restaurant and as we sat across from each other he rested his hand on his chin, eased into a smile and stared as I fumbled with my napkin feeling a little embarrassed. I asked him why he was looking at me. His smile was alive with affection and delight as he said plainly, I'm so glad to be here with you and spend time alone. I was totally taken off guard by his statement so I quickly changed the subject. I asked him about his new job and his fiancé and if they had finalized their wedding plans. A muscle quivered at his jaw and his mouth twisted as he cleared his throat and told me he had broken off their engagement soon after he returned from his trip to Miami. I didn't ask him why. He seemed as if he was holding back a raw emotion and needed someone to speak with. I reached my hand across the table and placed my hand on top of his. Eric in time this will pass. It's difficult in the beginning, but time does heal all wounds. In the back of my mind, I thought of how difficult it was for me to move past a heart-wrenching time in my life. Eric was speaking, but I was lost in my past. My mind burned with the memory of Ethan.

Eric looked at me across the table and blurted out that he had a confession to make.

"Jenna, the afternoon we spoke in your house I realized I was madly in love with you."

"Eric, what are you saying?" My head was swimming in confusion.

"I love you and want us to be together."

Disbelief took hold and silenced gripped me. How could he be in love with me and want to pursue a romantic relationship? I've known him since he was nine years old. He's twenty-four and I'm forty. I told him I didn't know how to feel about what he said. It took me completely off guard. He grabbed my hand and put it to his slightly parted lips.

"Jenna, promise me you'll think about it." "I've loved you my whole life and now I know I want you in my life forever."

He held my hand as we walked back to my hotel. I had to admit the warmth of his soft skin was intoxicating. I asked him if he would like to go to the bar in the restaurant for a drink before he left. He politely declined. He wanted me to think about what he spoke to me about. He asked if he could see me tomorrow before I left for the airport. As much as I thought it was wrong, I told him yes. He pressed his lips to mine, caressing my mouth more than kissing it. We would meet in

the morning at eleven-thirty. I found it very difficult to fall asleep. My mind wandered to what Eric had said to me. How could this possible that he
broke his engagement because of me? I tossed
and turned all night as I thought what a horrible
person, I must have been to get so attached to
him as a young boy.

Sunday morning as I sat in the hotel lobby
with my overnight bag at my side a few minutes
later Eric entered the hotel. I'm not sure if it was
because he announced he was in love the night
before with me, but as he came closer towards
me, I was focused on his tall muscular body and
compelling blue eyes. His smile was wide, his
teeth strikingly white as he approached me. As I
stood to greet him, he wrapped me in his arms
and placed a kiss on my lips as if his whole body
had been filled with love waiting for me. If it
hadn't been for the obvious factors, I would have
been equally attracted to him. We ate a late
breakfast and Eric couldn't keep his eyes off me
smiling that boyish grin I had grown to love.

"Well, have you given any thought to us?" as
he reached his hands across the table and held
mine in his.

"I do find you attractive, but it's hard for me
to separate Eric the boy, I knew, from Eric, the
man sitting across from me."

"Jenna, if you never knew my family how
would you feel about me?" "I'm not that nine-
year-old boy anymore, I'm a grown man who
loves you."

"It's very difficult for me to separate the two," I answered honestly. "I'm going to have to give this a lot of thought." "I'm just not sure if this will work out."

"Please, may I call you?" he begged. "I want to know you got home safely."

I told him he could text me, but please don't call. I needed time to think.

Before we departed, he asked me where my next signing was and I told in Dallas and the date. I didn't want him to ask Colleen in case she suspected Eric's questions about my book tours. We agreed not to talk to each other until next month. This would give me time to seriously think and I also told him he needed to think about this also. He told me he thought about me his whole life and he knew how much he loved me.

Chapter 8

The Uber driver dropped me home and I was anxious to get inside my house hoping not to be intercepted by Colleen. Unfortunately, that was not to be. Colleen had just left her house as she spotted me paying the driver.

"Hey girl," she said with excitement in her voice. "How was your trip?"

"It was so exciting." I was smiling from ear to ear. "I really felt so important like a famous author," laughing as I spoke.

"Did Eric get to see you?" "I told him where you would be and he said if he had the chance he would stop by."

With a flushed feeling traveling over my entire face I told her we did meet up and it was so good to see him. I hesitated in giving her too many details for fear of divulging too much information. I guess I was paranoid and didn't want her to read too much into what had transpired. I felt bad I lied to her, but how could I tell her the truth when I didn't even know what was going on between us.

That night I spent another sleepless night. I tossed and turned thinking about Eric's feelings towards me. He was hopelessly in love with me and wanted us to be together. My mind raced all night with thoughts of Eric; finally, somewhere in his future, he would realize this was a mistake. I knew I would be heartbroken. Just the possibility of never seeing him again would have broken my heart. If we remained friends would he still want to see me? I wished I could confide in Colleen, but that was not to happen. This was a decision I had to make on my own. I had to do a lot of souls searching to decide whether a relationship where there is sixteen years difference in age: I was forty; Eric in his late twenties would last. These questions plagued me day and night.

The following Saturday Colleen and I made a date to play tennis. I hoped the conversation would steer away from Eric. To my surprise, Colleen was giddy as a schoolgirl talking up a storm about her and Max. He kept pressuring her about marriage and she had to admit her defenses were slowing waning. Again, she asked me for my advice and again I told her to follow her heart.

I decided to write my second novel. I began writing the outline when Mark Harris called. After we exchanged greetings, he asked me when I thought my second novel would be completed. I told him I was just beginning the outline. He asked if we could possibly meet in person. He would get back to me soon since he was running late for a meeting. Mark made arrangements for us to meet in Los Angles He agreed to fly me out there, meet me at the airport and put me up in a hotel. What we needed to discuss would only take a day or two. I flew out on Monday morning and we would go to the Ritz-Carlton in downtown LA. I was somewhat at a disadvantage since I did not know what he looked like; however, he was able to recognize me from the photo on my book jacket. Mark was an above-average looking man with short blonde hair and a well-defined body. Muscles were all in the right places. He told me it was finally good to meet me in person. Sometimes you have an image in your mind of what the person you are conversing with looks like, but boy was I wrong. We grabbed an Uber and were quickly on our way to the hotel. Mark suggested we meet back in the lobby in an hour if that was all right with me. This was a business meeting and no time to relax. Mark met me at the front desk. I changed from my jeans into a pair of dress slacks and a tank top and short jacket. Mark looked very handsome in his black pants and Po-lo shirt. I must admit I was attracted to him for just a minute or two. During dinner, we discussed the topic of my new book and the time frame I was aiming for its completion. He said he would have all the necessary paperwork drawn up and ready for me to sign by late tomorrow afternoon. We said our good-byes and I told him I looked forward to seeing him tomorrow. I knew Eric worked somewhere downtown, but I hesitated in calling him. I still needed time to think. The meeting the following day went well and I agreed to have it completed by late next year.

Returning to Miami I was anxious to work on my outline. Colleen was again trying to fix me up with one of her or Max's friends. Finally, to get her to stop I lied and told her I was seeing my agent, Mark Harris. She was thrilled for me.

My Denver book signing was a week away. I finally texted Eric to let him know when I would arrive. I knew he would find out from his mother my travel plans and I didn't want Colleen to get suspicious. I still had not come to a decision about us and I hoped by telling him that he would give me more time. I didn't need the distraction. I just wanted to concentrate on my book sighing. As sweet and loving as he was, I needed more time to hash things out by myself.

The book signing was just as exciting as the first. My fans asked me when my next book would be on the store shelves, which brought a smile to my face. Signing and speaking to those who purchased my novel was a real high. I enjoyed every minute. After the signing, I was relieved to know that Eric had not shown up. Returning to my hotel late afternoon stood Eric. He greeted me with a warm hug and kiss on my lips as my body ached for more of his touch. I didn't want him here, but it became obvious to me the longer I was apart my love deepened and intensified for him. I was afraid of what I was getting myself into.

Please don't be angry with me, Jenna," he said as he slowly walked towards me. "One month of not being able to speak with you is more than I can bear."

"Eric," I said as I lovingly looked into his eyes that held me captivated, "I could never be angry with you."

It made me feel good and I was glad he was here. I became aware of his strength and the warmth of his flesh as he gathered me in his arms and held me snugly. We sat in the bar and ordered drinks and talked about his job and my book signing. I could see Eric was getting restless with all this talk. He wanted to know if I loved him the say way, he loved me. I buried my face in my hands and told him I questioned if our love would last. There were just too many factors that could go wrong and upset others.

"If you're talking about hurting my mother's feelings, you're wrong," his voice stern with an edge of hardness. "We're both adults and she has no say in my life and who I chose to fall in love with.

I moved next to him and sank into his comforting embrace. I enjoyed the feel of his arm around me. I tilted my head up towards his and whispered I loved him, but he had to promise that we take it slow, very slow. The smile that radiated from his face made him happy as he moved his lips over mine, devouring its softness. Whatever pace it would go he wanted me to be a part of his life.

Since it was dinnertime we decided to eat at the hotel's restaurant. Eric ordered a bottle of wine and we toasted to a new beginning for us. After I asked him if he would like to come to my room, to talk only. He agreed. As plans often go awry after thirty minutes of conversing Eric was holding me in his arms and placing his sort subtle lips on mine. I felt a shiver through my body as we sat on the bed. Is this the right way to feel about someone I had known so long? I needed to put the image of the young Eric out if my mind if I wanted this relationship to continue. I couldn't help but think what I was doing was wrong. My pleasure for him was pure and explosive. I gasped in agony as I desperately felt I needed more of him than just his touch. My whole body was flooded with desire and moan of ecstasy slipped through my lips. I realized where this was headed and I broke myself free from his warm pulsing body. I knew Eric wanted more and I apologized for letting it get this far. He caressed the side of my neck with his lips and declared I love you too much Jenna and I will be ready when you are. I never want to lose you. Eric left me that evening with feelings I thought I would never feel about him.

Chapter 9

Mark called a week later said he had business in Miami and would like to get together. I agreed to meet him, Coconut Grove, at the Mutiny hotel for lunch. We met in the hotel lobby and whisked me into the restaurant. We sat and chatted for a few minutes before he came right to the point.

"Jenna, I hope I'm not putting you on the spot, but are you seeing anyone?"

This came as a total surprise. He caught me off guard. I didn't want to tell him I was falling in love with my best friend's son who was quite a bit younger than me, so again I lied and told him I was not seeing anyone. He asked if he could see me again and I scrambled to come up with an excuse, which would not sound to flimsy. I told Mark he seemed like a very nice man, but right now I'm putting all my effort into writing my second book and I didn't have time for a long-distance relationship. He laughed and said he understood. He looked at me and said we never know what the future holds. As much as I liked him, I wasn't interested in him romantically. I feared if he knew the truth about me, he would think a lot less of me so I continued my lie.

Upon entering my hotel in Dallas on the third stop of my book signing I spotted Eric exiting the elevator. He usually met me at the bookstore. With a suitcase in tow, I walked towards him wondering why he would be in the hotel before me. In one forward motion, I was in his arms locked into his embrace. He pressed my lips with a relentless enjoyment and I was wrapped in a cocoon of euphoria. Eric grabbed my suitcase and we ascended to my room on the sixth floor. I was curious how he knew my suite number. He told me he reserved the room next to me and wanted to spend as much time with me as he could, so he reserved the adjacent room. I told him it was fine with me, however, I was a little shocked by his boldness. I placed my keycard into the door and when the light appeared green Eric opened the door and I stepped into the room. I told him I was a little tired and maybe a shower would make me feel better hoping he would retreat to his room and give me some privacy. No problem he replied as he removed the TV remote from the desk and began scrolling the program guide. He asked me if I would mind if he sat on the bed and watch TV while I showered. A little annoyed and also with laughter in my voiced I smiled at him and said of course and make yourself at home.

Totally confused by his behavior I opened my suitcase and hung up the few clothes I brought. I laid a pair of sweat pants and a short T-shirt, which exposed my midriff on the bathroom sink and took a shower. Leaving the bathroom Eric's eyes were fixed on me.

"Wow, Jenna, I've never seen you dressed like this!" "You look as sexy as hell." as his smile broadened with approval.

Feeling slightly embarrassed I crawled on the left side of the bed next to Eric. I grabbed my laptop, which was on the nightstand next to me and placed it between my legs and began to scroll to various news sites. Slowly Eric inched his body closer toward mine. I felt his strong hard body next to mine. It took all my strength to keep my eyes on the computer screen. Suddenly I felt his hand move up and down my arm. I shivered with desire. Don't make a move I told myself. I kept my eyes glued to the screen. I finally settled back and enjoyed the feel of his skin on mine. His touch was firm and persuasive and invited more, and before I knew it, I was asleep in the circle of his arms.

"Well hello sleepyhead," he said, as he as his gaze traveled over my face.

"Why didn't you wake me?" "What time is it?"

"You were tired and I didn't want to wake you." "I told you I wanted to spend as much time with you as I could even if it meant watching you sleep," he said with a chuckle in his voice.

Eric tilted my head gently toward his and placed his sensuous lips on mine. I had to fight the overwhelming need to be close to him as his gaze riveted on my face and then moved over my body slowly. Releasing myself from his trance I suggested we get ready for dinner. He agreed and left my room and we agreed to meet downstairs in forty-five minutes. Oh my god, I thought. What am I getting myself into?

Eric was already at the bar when I arrived. We moved to a table in the corner of the room. He looked so handsome in his navy-blue pants and a button-down cream-colored shirt. I had to admit he was irresistible. I'm sure there are plenty of young women at work who would love to get their hands all over him. Why did he love me? That was a thought that plagued me constantly. I was afraid of again losing someone whom I loved and meant the world to me. We sat across from each other and Eric leaned forward and held my hand and asked me if I had given thought to our relationship. I shared with my concerns about our age difference and most important his mother's reaction and acceptance of us. Again, he reminded me as his lips pressed together in anger. He didn't care if his mother disapproved. She would have to come to terms with the fact that we loved each other and wanted to spend the rest of our lives together. It was not easy for me to lose my best friend. She had been there for me during my darkest time. I couldn't do this to her. I couldn't jeopardize our friendship. Eric was waiting for an answer but all I could shake my head indicating I didn't know. How could I tell her I was falling desperately in love with her son?

Chapter 10

Mark called more frequently making excuses for why we needed to get together to discuss business. I knew we could do everything by fax or Skyping if necessary. I made excuses that I was busy working on my new book and didn't want to interrupt my creative streak. I guess he believed me because his calls soon faded off, however, I felt he had not given up quite yet.

I pushed myself to work long hard hours to complete my book. My mind flashed many times to Eric, to us, to our future together. I asked myself a million times did I think this relationship has a future? I knew I was in love with Eric. Would our love be able to withstand Colleen's wrath and disappointment in me? The more as the days past by I missed Eric tremendously. The last leg of my tour was in two weeks and I looked forward to seeing Eric. The New York City book signing was in Times Square. I was booked at the Sheraton Hotel. I knew Eric would be there and for the first time, I yearned for his presence.

I took the Uber from Kennedy airport to the hotel. I registered and hoped I would again see Eric as he emerged from the elevator. Unfortunately, he was nowhere in sight. Just as I entered my room, I received a text from Eric. His plane was delayed and he didn't know how long he before he arrived. He said it would most likely be late and not to wait to eat dinner with him He told me he would see me when he got to the hotel. I texted him back and said, see you soon. It was almost seven-thirty. I waited for Eric despite what he said. A knock on the door startled me as I finished texting. Could it be him? I opened the door with a smile that sent my pulse racing. It was from Mark. I guess the expression on my face showed my disappointment. Mark apologized for showing up unexpectedly and told me he was here finishing up some business that had taken him longer than expected. I no longer knew when he was telling me the truth or not. I had to believe him he was my agent. He asked me if I had eaten dinner yet. I told him I hadn't. He asked me to join him and even though I didn't want to I was famished and Eric would not arrive until very late. I became slightly annoyed when we approached our table, which was in the middle of the restaurant. It was covered on white linen cloth with two lighted candles and a bouquet of roses, which suggested something more than a spur of the moment dinner. I tried to keep the conversation light and amusing. I didn't want the focus to again become about the possibility of there being an us. I tried thought out dinner not to show my annoyance and ate my meal with a forced smile on my face. Mark wanted to order dessert I felt to keep us here longer, but I told him I was full and needed to get back to my room. I thanked him for dinner and retreated to my room.

I sat on the bed worried now where he could possibly be. It was already midnight. I decided to back downstairs and wait for him. As I exited the elevator and passed the bar there sat Eric. I walked up behind him and placed my hand gently on his shoulder. I asked him how long he had been sitting here. As he began to speak, I could smell the alcohol on his breath and his eyes seemed to be red from tears. His voice broke in a tear-smothered whisper. He had been here for three hours. When he texted, me he was already in the hotel hoping to surprise me. He knocked in my door and when I didn't answer he came down to the lobby. That was when he saw Mark and I sitting at the table, which appeared to be a romantic evening. With a tremor of fear in his voice, he said he thought I had found someone else. The two of you looked to be enjoying each other's company and I didn't want to interfere. I looked lovingly into his eyes, the eyes I knew I loved so much and kissed him on his lips and in a low and smooth voice I told him he was my agent. He was finalizing business here and stopped by to say hello. I only accepted a dinner invitation with him because you were arriving late and told me not to wait for you. He responded with a trace of laughter in his voice and reminded himself that he did tell me that.

Eric got up from the barstool and grabbed me tightly. He told me he didn't know what he would do if I found someone else. I assured him that my relationship was Mark was strictly business and he had nothing to worry about. I loved him and only him. I asked Eric if had booked the room next to me. He said he did. I asked him if he would like to stay in my room for the remainder of our stay. A sexy smile emerged from his face. Let's get going he insisted. He wanted to move his things into my room ASAP. We walked back to our rooms with his arm wrapped so tightly around me, as if he was going to lose me. Eric moved all his belongings into my room in record time. I had to laugh. I didn't think anyone could move as fast as he did. Once he got settled in my suite I told him I wanted to shower. He was watching TV as I plunged myself into the tub instead. It felt so relaxing and for the first time, I was at peace with myself. I walked into the bedroom where Eric was on top of the comforter. Walking over to him in my sheer lace lavender Teddy I straddled myself over him as he sat in his silk black boxers with his legs crossed at his ankles. Before I could reposition myself, Eric was on top of me. I didn't resist when his hands slipped off my Teddy. His hands rested on my bare breasts and I felt the hardness of his chest crush against my breasts. I sensed the thrill of his arousal as we lay skin to skin. Heat rippled under my skin as we recognized the flush of sexual desire, we both had been feeling for months. Our breaths came in long, surrendering moans as we aroused a passion in each other that only grew stronger. We surrendered completely to each other and we savored the feelings of satisfaction between both of us. We laid in each other's arms fully satisfied with what we had been longing from each other. Leaning on my elbow I ran my fingers playfully down his face. I pleaded with him to promise me his mother not know about us. I promise I would tell Colleen when I felt the time was right. Eric refused to keep us a secret and told me so as he planted tiny sensuous kisses on my neck. I pushed him away and told him I was serious. I would let her know soon. His desire for me overrode everything I had said and again we were entwined into each other. His lips traced a sensuous path to ecstasy as we brought pleasure to each other again. We awoke in each other's arms and as much as we wanted to enjoy each other again we both had to get ready to leave. We decided to meet on alternate weekends either in Miami or Los Angles. I was on cloud nine. My reluctance for being with Eric had vanished and I was now totally committed to him.

****

I now had to decide when to tell Colleen. I knew I should have told her a while ago, but I knew something as shocking as this would be the end of our friendship. Eric and I met in Coconut Grove and were staying for the weekend at the Mutiny Hotel. According to him his mom never went to the Grove anymore. She had been there a few times and decided the traffic in getting there wasn't worth the trip. One afternoon Eric and I were walking along Bayside and decided to have lunch in one of the outdoor cafes overlooking the bay. We later found out Max was meeting with a client and spotted us walking hand and hand, planting kisses on each other in a sensuous way. I don't think he objected to what he was seen, but he related it to Colleen.

Living my life now being in love with a wonderful man I didn't think life could get any better. A sudden banging on my door interrupted my thoughts. I looked through the peephole and saw Colleen standing there.

"Hi, Colleen," "What's up?" I asked with a smile on my face.

"How dare you?" "How could you?" "I thought you and I were friends?" she screamed in a high–pitched voice.

She pushed past me and went into the kitchen, her back against the sink.

"What the hell were you thinking?" "Max saw you and Eric in Bayside and told me the two of you acted more like lovers than friends. Tears were streaming down her reddened face.

I approached her, but she walked away from me.

"Colleen, I'm so sorry." "I wanted to tell you, but I didn't know how."

"How and when did all this happen?" she demanded.

Not knowing where to begin I thought I was best to start at the beginning. I told Colleen when Eric visited me last time in Miami after he graduated from college, he told me he was in love with me, but I didn't take him seriously. He showed up at my first book signing in LA and it there again he said he loved me. He's met me at all the other signings and now we meet each other either here or in Los Angles.
You knew my son was off limits to you. You're the adult here not him.

"Are you having sex with him?" she asked, her eyes bulging out of her head. "Of course you are!" "How stupid of me to even ask."

She told me she was disappointed and very angry with me and there was no way we could ever be friends.

"You're nothing but a whore, a pervert and a bitch," she screamed, her eyes swollen with tears.

With these hateful words she stormed out of my house slamming the door behind her. I sat on my couch weeping uncontrollably. What have I done? My cell phone rang. The caller ID indicated it was from Eric. I couldn't answer his call. He called and texted me several times throughout the day. The calls went to voice mail, the texts I never answered. I remained on my couch ashamed of my feelings for Eric and how much I had hurt and destroyed my very best friend. After all, Colleen had done for me how could I have betrayed her the way I did. She had always been there for me as any good friend would have and I destroyed her trust. I should have never given into Eric's advances. She was right, I was the adult in this situation. I should have just walked away and never let him into my life. Eric was persistent in calling me well into the night, but I refused to answer his calls. I needed to rethink my relationship with him. I would call him in the morning; hopefully, I would have sorted out all this madness and destruction I had caused.

The next morning as I was about to dial Eric's cell my phone rang. It was him in a frantic voice he told me he was trying to get in touch with me since yesterday and was worried something terrible had happened to me. With tears choking my voice and barely able to speak I recounted what had transpired between his mother and me. Eric wanted to call his mother, but I insisted the feud was between Colleen and me. She would always take his side. I was the evil one, the villain. I was the cradle snatcher, the person who preyed on her son since he was nine. I knew she was upset and shocked, but the vile and hideous names she called me were more than I could bear. My heart was broken into a million pieces and I knew it would never be repaired. I told Eric I needed time to think about what I had done to his mother and our friendship. He agreed to leave me alone and call me tomorrow.

I gave serious thought to all the hurt I had caused and decided it was best to call Eric and end our relationship. It was a heart-wrenching decision, but I knew it was for the best. It broke my heart to know I would never see him again. That evening I called him.

"Hi Eric," I said as my stomach clenched tight.

"Hi, sweetheart." "Are you feeling any better today?" he asked and I could almost see the love and hurt in his eyes as he spoke to me.

"Eric, I know I am going to upset you by what I have to say, but I have decided it's for the best that we stop seeing each other." Tears were streaming down my face as I spoke these words. I knew my words stabbed him in his heart.

"Jenna, are you saying you are no longer in love with me." "I can't believe what you said is true." "I know we love each other." His voice growing still and serious.

He pleaded with me not to end our relationship. He loved me with all his heart and he knew I felt the same way he did. He knew his mother was the only one who had a problem with our relationship. Even Adam was on board with us being together. His admission about his brother shocked me. It was too late. He begged me not to be too hasty in my decision. I suggested we not see each other for a while. He agreed as long as it meant we would see each other soon. He would only keep in touch with me by text. I agreed. Since Eric lived in California it might be easier if I learned to be by myself. Before we ended our conversation, he told me he would be traveling on company business for the next two months. I welcomed the distance it would put between us. It would give me time to do some serious soul searching.

Chapter 11

Luckily, I had my new book to occupy my time. I decided before I sent it to my editor, I would review it again. I reread it several more times and spend the next few weeks as I read and reread it from cover to cover something, I had learned from Professor Williams. Writing is a process he told me. I had to be patient in knowing the book was completed. I was absorbed in my book, but my mind never strayed far from Eric. Absence is supposed to make the heart grow fonder, but I hoped it would be the reverse for me. I loved him and knew he would never be forgotten. I tried my best to get him out of my heart.

Lately, I had begun to feel tired and needed to nap in the afternoons, something I had never done before. After two weeks of still feeling listless, I decided to see my doctor. I convinced myself it was stress from all I had been going through. The doctor ran all the usual tests. She left the examining room and my mind immediately reverted back to my mom. Fear gripped my heart as I remembered her symptoms: extreme fatigue, and lack of energy. I'm too young I thought, but so was she. The fear of cancer consumed my thoughts. When the doctor re-entered the room, I didn't give her a chance to speak. I blurred out do I have cancer? As she took, he seat behind her desk she smiled and asked me why on earth had I come to that conclusion? You're five weeks pregnant she told me. I shook my head in total disbelief. I asked her again if she was positively sure. Again, with a smile on her face, she confirmed one hundred percent, I was pregnant. She said she needed to see me again in two weeks. I was considered to be at high risk due to my age, forty-one. She congratulated me as I tried to force a smile on my face, my head in a fog. From that point on I had no idea what she said to me. I walked to the reception area and made my next appointment. Oh my god, I thought. How could this be? I was never able to conceive with Ethan and now I was going to be a mother. I was both elated and stressed. I had to tell Eric. My time to think about us sent me into a tailspin. What if he decided to find someone closer to his age? I was the one who pushed him away. If he fell in love with someone else, I couldn't disrupt his life. I decided if that were so, I would raise our child by myself. I still had time to let him know about the baby. I decided to wait.

I was now seven weeks pregnant and I felt like I was going to die. My morning sickness was so severe it left me lying in bed most of the day and barely able to keep anything in my stomach. My two-week appointment couldn't come soon enough. I told the doctor how badly I felt and she assured me what I was suffering from was Hyperemesis gravid arum. Its symptoms included excessive vomiting and nausea and it could possibly last my entire pregnancy. I still had not heard from Eric. I sent him several texts. He must be still out of the country on business. Again, my mind raced to him having found someone else and not having any time for me. If this was the case, he deserved to be happy with someone new. I decided I would tell him he was not responsible for this baby in any way. I would be the responsible one. I would not put this responsibility on him. I was now two months pregnant and my morning sickness had not improved. Nausea and vomiting were debilitating.

I noticed a few days age Colleen's car never left the driveway and her inside house lights were on a cycle of going on and off at the same time day and night. I guessed she was not home; perhaps she was spending time with Max, now that we were no longer friends. I was all alone. My best friend, the only one close enough to call my sister was out of my life forever.

****

One particular Sunday morning my nausea was so severe I sat in my bad with my back against the headboard. Dressed in a flimsy sleeveless nightgown my hair in a ponytail pulled away from my face so the vomit didn't get caught in my loose strands of hair whenever I was face down in the toilet bowl. A wet towel was never far away from me. It had become my new blankly. It was my companion. I didn't go anywhere with it. Looking my best was not my top priory anymore. Trying to get through the day was all I yearned, hoped and prayed for. Each new day brought a slight bit of relief. I had no idea how to get through this all by myself but I had to. I was in this by myself.

I started to doze off when I thought I heard the front doorbell followed by a knock on the door. Prying myself out of bed, not before wiping my face with the wet towel. I slowly walked down the hallway with each hand plastered against the walls to balance myself. Another wave of nausea hit and I had to stop to steady myself. The knocking on the door now became louder and louder. I tried to tell whomever it was I was coming but all my energy was to get to the door. Struggling to look out the peephole I saw Eric. I opened the door and the horrified look on his face confirmed my exact thought of what I must look like.

"Jenna, you look terrible?" "What's wrong?"

I didn't have the strength or courage to answer him. I opened the door wider and indicated for him to come in. Before he could say anything more, I raced to the bathroom, sat on my knees with my head leaning against the toilet. Eric followed close behind. After several minutes I pulled myself off the bathroom floor and returned to my bed. The look on Eric's face was full of fear.

"Eric, why are you here?' I asked embarrassed that he had to be a witness to all this.

"It doesn't matter why I'm here." "What's wrong, Jenna, you're scaring me."

I lied and told him I had been sick for a few days with the flu and he should probably leave before he gets sick also. He was not leaving. He returned from the kitchen with a cup of hot tea for me and told me to drink some. I might feel better with some fluids in me. Little did he know the tea would probably have me racing to the bathroom again. I asked him to just leave it on the nightstand I would drink some later when it cooled off. I asked him why he was here in Miami. He joined me sitting carefully on the edge of the bed. With apprehension in his voice, he told me his mother and Max were married on Saturday and they left this morning on a ten-day honeymoon cruise. His words ripped through my heart. Colleen hated me so much she never told me she was getting married. Tears blinded my eyes and chocked my voice. I asked Eric about the wedding. He told me he didn't attend. If his mother couldn't accept me as part of his life, he didn't want to be part of her new life. As I heard this, I felt so much anger with myself for getting between Eric and his Mom. Adam and his family were in attendance and so were Max's children and their families. I never wanted it to come to this. I wouldn't allow Eric to have to choose between his mother and me.

"Eric please don't do this," I begged. Your mother loves you and I'm sure she was heartbroken that you were not there." "She is only looking out for you."

"Jenna, I told you I love you, you're my life and I want us to be together." "If she can't accept you as part of my life then that's her decision.

Eric leaned closer toward me and planted a warm and tender kiss on my forehead. His hands were soft and gentle as they cascaded down my arms and that's when his hand rested on my small round belly. His hand slowly caressed my stomach. With a smile of pure euphoria on his face he announced, we're pregnant. He never doubted for one second that the baby wasn't his. In an affectionate whisper, he asked me why I was going to tell him. I told him I wanted to let him know, he had every right to know, but I didn't want to tie him down with the responsibility of being a parent. I was more than happy if I had to raise the baby by myself.

"Jenna, I couldn't be happier." "I finally have everything I ever wanted."

I saw the joy and happiness that emanated from his face as he crawled into bed next to me and held me in his arms. I explained my condition to him and he told me he would make an appointment the following day and the two of us would speak with the doctor. We were in this together and he was going to be there for me starting today. Just his thoughtful and loving words made me know I was truly in love with him.

I explained my condition to Eric and could see the pain and hurt in his eyes as sadness etched on his face knowing I had to go through all of this alone. He wanted to take me back to California with him so he could be involved in every step of my care. I couldn't love him any more than I could think possible.

Two days later we were meeting with my doctor. Eric bombarded her with a slew of questions concerning the baby and me. He wanted to take me back home with him and she agreed it would be better if I had someone with me for the sake of the baby just in case, I was having a bad day, which she assured us should be getting better as my pregnancy progressed.

Leaving the office Eric filled me in on his plans. We would stay in Miami long enough to pack up whatever I needed to take with me. I decided to call Professor William's daughter, Linda, and ask her to keep an eye on my house while I was in LA. She arrived the next day and giving her the house keys I reminder her to please bring her children over so they could use the pool. All of the other details for the house to remain empty Eric handled. I only brought a few suitcases and my writing materials. I prayed the five-hour flight would not have me running to the cramped plane bathrooms. The thought of that made me queasy. The wonderful man who was so loving and thoughtful booked us in first class. He thought I would be more comfortable and there would be fewer people seated near us. He was a genuinely compassionate and wonderful man and he was mine. Eric was very attentive the entire trip always asking if I was doing ok, did I need anything. As much as I loved him, I didn't want to tell him I would feel better if he didn't ask so many questions. At times I was very uncomfortable. I wish I could have stuck my head out of the plane's window just for some fresh air. I knew better than to say anything to Eric because he was more nervous for me than I was. He was committed to doing the best he could to make me feel as comfortable as possible.

As we disembarked from the plans Eric asked if I needed assistance getting our luggage and to the cab. A wheelchair he suggested. Trying to hold back my laughter I looked him square in the face and told him I'm pregnant not ninety years old. He reached over to me with his arm around my waist, kissed me on the top of the head and just laughed. Reaching out to me he laced his fingers with mine and we walked through the concourse. The fresh air felt wonderful as it encircled my sweaty face and I started to feel more refreshed.

****

A Lincoln Towne car pulled up in front of us. The driver got out of the car, greeted Eric and proceeded to place our luggage in the trunk. As we sat in the back, I asked Eric why all the fanfare. The first-class tickets and now a limousine. Turning his head toward me with a smile on his lips he said it was one of the perks of his new position. He had been promoted to Chief Operating Officer. He was responsible for the day-to-day operations of the corporation he worked for. I was so proud of him as I nuzzled myself closer to his side. I knew he worked very hard to get to where he was today. I noticed we missed the exit for LA and were heading south. Again, another surprise as he told me we would be living in Santa Monica. He had received his promotion two months ago. He bought a five thousand square foot condo with four bedrooms and three baths. It also had an office for me to do my writing. His handsome face looked at me as his fingers stroked my face and whispered in my ear. I always knew you would be mine. I touched his lips with a soft playful finger and then gave his lower lip a hungry nibble. Don't start things he said we can't finish as he looked at me and the double meaning of his gaze was obvious.

Looking upward to the gigantic tower as we exited the car Eric told me his condo was located on the sixteenth floor overlooking the ocean. Riding the elevator to my new home his arm curled around my protruding belly and he placed his chin on the top of my head. He expressed how fortunate he felt to have me finally, all his. Climbing upward to his apartment he briefly told me details of what it was like. It was four thousand five hundred square feet with four bedrooms and a designated room for me to continue my writing. Exiting the elevator, we walked down the hall wall and before he removed his keys from his pocket, he held me close and told me he loved me and then planted a soft kiss on my lips. As we entered, the most breathtaking view of the Pacific Ocean captured my eyes. He took me on a grand tour and it was too overwhelming, to say the least. The kitchen, family room, and master bedroom all had a panoramic view of the ocean. He told me his plan was for us to always be together and hopefully raise a family together. I was speechless. I guess I was just shocked at how much he truly loved me.

It was two weeks after I arrived at my new home when Eric decided it was time, he told his mother about us. He wanted to make the phone call in private to spare me his mother's wrath, but I insisted I wanted to be by his side when he made the call. Seated next to him on the couch he dialed Colleen's cell phone number. Sitting so close to him I could hear her phone ringing. After three rings I could hear her voice loud and clear as she spoke. Eric asked his mother details about her wedding, thinking this would soften the blow.

She was quick to let him know how disappointed she was that he did not attend their wedding. He, in turn, cut that part of the conversation off and changed the subject to their honeymoon cruise.

"Mom, I have great news." He said smiling ear to ear and pressing my hand.

" You broke up with that tramp!" She replied sarcastically.

" Mom, if you are going to speak like that, I'm going to hang up," Eric answered with a fierce look of anger on his face.

"What is your great news sweetheart?"

"Jenna and I are pregnant!" "You're going to be a grandmother!"

"That slut trapped you." I could hear the disgust in her voice as my heart slowly sank.

"She couldn't get pregnant by Ethan so she trapped you."

"I can't believe you would let her do this to you." "I thought you were smarter than this." "She always wanted a baby and now she got her to wish." "I hope you can convince her to have an abortion."

Eric refused to allow his mother to continue her conversation. He told her this was real and if she refused to come to terms with everything, she would be the one who missed out on his life.

Colleen's words ripped a hole in my heart as I slowly got up from the couch and headed toward the bedroom. I closed the door and lay on the bed and wept feeling like I was solely responsible for all of this turmoil between Eric and his mother. I couldn't fathom how much she hated me.

Eric entered our bedroom and sat on the edge of the bed. Wrapping his arms around me he told me he was so sorry for his mother's harsh words. His only concern was for our baby and me.

Chapter 12

The remainder of my pregnancy improved. It had eased up but I still experienced intermittent bouts of nausea. I exercised daily walking around the neighborhood. I never ventured too far from home for fear of possibly having to vomit. I wanted the comfort of my own toilet to throw up in, not the street.

Eric texted me every day to check up on me and when he was in meetings all day, he made sure his secretary called me. He was so protective of me I sometimes found myself laughing at his over cautiousness. To him, I was this fragile human being caring our baby and he would protect us come hell or high water.

In the last three weeks of my pregnancy, Eric decided to work from home. He wanted to spend as much time with me before the baby arrived. It was a welcome relief for me to have him here with me. Emerging from his office one afternoon he told me he just got off the phone with Max. I placed the magazine I was reading down on the couch next to me. Eric sat cuddled close to me hugging me as he spoke. He repeated the conversation he had with Max. Max wanted to apologize for telling Colleen about seeing the two of us in Coconut Grove that fateful day. He felt if he hadn't said anything to Colleen maybe none of this dissension would have occurred. Eric assured Max that his mother's reaction would probably be the same regardless of how she found out. Max confided in Eric that he was fine with our relationship. You can't plan who you are going to fall in love with he said. He asked if the next time he was in California he could stop by; he would love to see us. Of course, Eric told him that he and his mom were welcome here anytime.

Feeling more energetic and more like my old self, I decided to go to the nearby mall and do some window-shopping. Just before I was ready to leave my phone rang. It was from Eric. He asked how I was feeling and I joyfully told him my plans for the morning. Just hearing the happiness in his voice made me feel like I was on cloud nine. He called to let me know he wanted to take me out to dinner and while I was going to be shopping to buy myself a new dress. He wanted me to look my very best and feel beautiful.

Eric arrived home at his usual time at 6:30 and found me in the bedroom rummaging through my closet. Haphazardly thrown across the bed were at least a have a dozen outfits I had tried on and tossed aside.

"Hey, what's going on?" Eric's expression was more playful than serious.

"I can't find one dress that doesn't make me look like I'm ten times bigger than I really am. " I cried with tears rolling down my cheeks in pure frustration.

Standing in my bra and panties with my belly protruding, Eric walked up behind me and placed his hands around my waist. Just his touch sent sparks to my body in all the right places. He placed his face between my neck and shoulders planting gentle kisses on my neck.

"Babe, whatever you wear I'm going to love you in it; besides you're supposed to look pregnant."

Even though that compliment didn't help my ego I don't think most women want to look fat but pregnant women were supposed to have a certain glow. Somehow, I felt robbed of that magical aura.

Turning around to face my knight in shining armor Eric slid his fingers sensuously over my arms sending a lusty feeling of warmth all over me.
His lips were a hint of what he wanted and it was me.

"Jenna, sweetheart," he said with a devilish grin, "I need to change into a different suit and since you're not dressed yet would you be up for a little…. He didn't need to finish his sentence. We hadn't been intimating in months and now I was yearning for him to be close to me, inside of me. Lust became an overpowering and devouring obsession. I couldn't control myself as I fumbled to unbuckle his belt and began loosening his tie. Reaching for the zipper to his pants we both tumbled onto the bed and laughed lie two teenagers. He eased off my bra and panties and swept me in his arms as our lips met, he claimed my mouth with a savage kiss. My body felt his hunger, as our tongues tasted each other with a savage desire. Our bodies were on fire with a pure explosion of pleasure.

We arrived at the restaurant a few minutes past our reservation time but making love with Eric was better than any dinner. He was my appetizer, main course, and dessert. The maître d escorted us to a booth in the back of the restaurant away from the other patrons. The table was elegantly covered with a white linen tablecloth and napkins and silver utensils placed perfectly on either side of the white China plates. The centerpiece was an elegant crystal vase containing long stem red roses. As I squeezed myself between the seat and the table Eric sat across from me. He reached for my hand and laced his fingers with mine. Read the card he said with a boyish grin. I removed the card and stared at him intently before opening it.

To my two most precious gifts in my world. I will always love you.
Love, Eric, and Daddy. A tear escaped and rolled down my cheek as I read the card. I just felt so blessed to have such a wonderful man in my life. I told him how much I loved him and I was the luckiest woman in the world to have someone like him. His response was that he was the lucky one.

We dined on lobster, wild rice and a Caesar salad. The waiter returned to the table after a while to take our dessert order. Eric told him we wanted to wait a short while. I stared into Eric's eyes still not believing how much we loved one another. I noticed he seemed kind of fidgety and asked him if everything was okay. He slid out of his seat, faced me and balancing himself on one knee he fumbled inside his jacket pocket.

From a small black velvet box, Eric removed a four-carat pear-shaped diamond ring.

"Jenna you are my world. I love you and never want to live without you." "Will you marry me?"

Being caught completely off guard I brought both hands to my mouth and now crying uncontrollably I just kept shaking my head yes, too emotional to speak.

"You know how much I love you and I want to be your wife."

Eric kissed me gently on my lips as he sat back in his seat. So how soon before we get married, he asked excitedly? I told him I wanted to wait until after the baby was born and I wanted to look my very best on my wedding day. I needed to lose the baby weight. He agreed but made me promise him we would be married no later than six months after the baby was born. I agreed. He swore if I was going to postpone the date, he would kidnap me and drag me to City Hall.

I was already in my ninth month and prayed the baby would be just as eager as I was to enter the world soon. We chose two names, Christopher and Olivia.

The exciting day finally arrived while I was making breakfast. My water broke and the contractions were starting to begin. I called for Eric who was in the shower and he quickly got dressed and helped me clean myself up. He retrieved a pair of sweat pants and a t-shirt for me to wear.

We arrived at the hospital in record time constantly reminding him to slow down. I was immediately admitted and brought to the birthing suite. The room was bright and cozy with a large screen TV, a large sofa and silk plants aligning the walls. I guessed the décor was supposed to take your mind off of the pain while you screamed through each contraction. Why the TV was there I had no idea.

I was in labor for nine hours and Eric coached me every step of the way. Many times, I yelled and screamed at him just out of pain and tiredness. Each time he kissed my forehead and told me how much he loved me. With my final push, I gave birth to a beautiful, healthy, seven-pound little girl. Our Olivia was finally here in my arms. She had black hair and beautiful blues eyes just like her daddy. Eric was beyond ecstatic. I had never seen him so happy. He followed the nurses around never taking his eyes off our precious gift. When she was finally cleaned up the nurse placed her in the middle of my chest and I immediately fell in love with this tiny beauty we had created. Sometime later Eric told me he had called his brother who sent his love and congratulations to us both. Eric hoped this good news would soften his mother, but when he called her with the good news she handed her phone to Max. I knew Eric was hurt and disappointed by his mother's reaction, but he would not let it distract from the happiness of our blessed event.

I was released from the hospital the following day. Eric insisted I hire a nurse to help with the nightly feedings so I could get some rest. This was one subject there would be no compromising with. I had waited so long to be a mom I was not going to miss one moment of changing diapers, feedings in the middle of the night and being downright tired all the time.

Eric was a wonderful dad. Many nights he got up to feed the baby and change her diaper. He loved his little girl and she was sure becoming a daddy's girl. He was a hands-on dad in every sense of the word. Coming home from work his first priority was our daughter. He set aside time to play with her, read to her, give her a bath and put her to bed. Not only was he an exceptional man, but he was also an exceptional dad.

Chapter 13

As the six- month deadline was approaching Eric was a constant reminder as to when and where we were going to marry. I was back down to my original weight and sometimes I had to confess as much as I loved him maybe getting married was not the right thing to do. Plenty of women raise their children as a single parent with the support of the father. I was almost twice his age and maybe I was being unfair to tie him down. I knew discussing this with him would be a no-win for me, but it was a constant thought that was on my mind. I knew I needed to stop thinking this way. I loved him with all my heart and I knew he loved me also and raising our daughter together was our first priority.

We decided a small wedding with Adam and his family and his mom and Max would suffice. The wedding would be officiated by a minister friend of Eric's with a reception at the Capo Restaurant where Eric proposed. In a size six, cream-colored strapless form-fitted gown and a spray of yellow roses clipped to the back of my French braid I stood at the entrance of the small chapel gazing at the handsome man in a navy-blue suit. His eyes were fixed on me as I made my way toward him. We exchanged our vows both with tears in our eyes. The minister pronounced us husband and wife and told Eric he could now kiss his bride. The smile in his eyes contained a sensuous flame as his mouth curved into a smile and as his lips were placed on mine and told me without words how much he loved me.

Colleen, of course, did not attend and Max constantly apologized for her. Max took plenty of wedding photos. Several of Eric, the baby and me. A few pictures of us by ourselves. I had to think he wanted to show Colleen how happy we were and of course to show her a picture of Olivia. The reception soon came to an end and it was heartbreaking when such a happy occasion was over and we all had to say our good-byes. Kisses and hugs were exchanged as we went our separate ways

We arrived home and I put Olivia in her crib for the night. I began to undress and I felt a pair of warm and tender lips on my neck. I turned around and Eric was holding a beautiful heart-shaped diamond necklace in his hands. He unhooked the clasp and placed the necklace around my neck.

"It's beautiful Eric," I said as I kissed his sexy plump lips.

"I think it's time for our honeymoon." "Are you too tired?" he asked as he gently ran his index finger across my lower lip.

"Never for you sweetheart." "I'm yours whenever and forever."

We slowly undressed each other. Picking me up in his arms he placed me gently down on the bed. He claimed my mouth with a savage kiss.

Where his lips touched me my body it came alive. He placed his fingers in my mouth, teasing them along with his tongue. I felt a tiny prick of his teeth against my neck filling me and fueling my desire. This was the ultimate pleasure. My body was on fire as his toned and muscular body was on top of me. With burning bodies and molten hearts, our bodies became one. Waking up the next morning with Eric's muscular arm wrapped around my waist I knew I was the luckiest woman on earth.

Olivia was growing like a weed and I decided it was time to shop for some new clothes for her. I told Eric about my plans and he suggested we meet for lunch at a café near his office at 12:30. I drove to a trendy section of Santa Barbara. The streets were lined on both sides with high-end boutique shops. I would never have thought of spending an excessive amount of money on clothing for myself but this was for Olivia and I wanted only the best for her. I lost track of time when I began searching through all the adorable clothes for little girls. I suddenly remember to look at my watch it was already 11:30 and I needed to decide on a purchase and be on my way. I chose a pink and white polka dot dress for Olivia. I made my purchase and hurried to my car.

I made my way onto the left lane of the highway and the only thing I remembered is the light turned green and from out of nowhere a car was racing towards me sending my car into a spin. I hit the median and that was my last memory.

Eric was waiting for us and we were already thirty minutes late. He started to worry and just about to call me when a police car pulled up to the restaurant. Eric sensed something was not right and approached the officer. The concerned look on his face directed the officer to ask if he was Eric Barnett. He said he retrieved Eric's name from my phone under ICE, in case of emergency, and guessed by the same last names there was some connection and called his office which was also displayed. He informed Eric that there had been an accident. The baby only sustained minor injuries but the woman was in critical condition. That was all the information he had to give Eric along with the name of the hospital.

Eric raced to the hospital and first checked on Olivia who looked like a sleeping angel in the hospital crib. The nurses assured him she would be fine. He then hurried to my room where he found me hooked up to wires attached to beeping machines. There I lay, lifeless in a coma. He held my hand and kissed my lips begging me to wake up. Olivia and he needed them. After a few hours, he decided to call Adam and his mother.

"Max I'm so worried about Jenna." "I don't know what I will do if I lost her."

"Calm down son." "Colleen and I will take the first available flight out." "It's time your mother stopped acting like a jilted teenager and more like your mother."

Some part of Eric was relieved that his mom would be there to comfort him. He needed her and wanted her to be close by him.

Eric sat by my bedside only leaving for a few minutes at a time to check on Olivia. One of the nurses told him, Olivia was in good hands and it might be better if he stayed with me in case I woke up and He would be the first face I saw when I woke up.

Two o'clock in the morning Max and Colleen arrived at the hospital. They found Eric asleep in the chair next to my bed holding my limp hand. Colleen walked quietly up to Eric and kissed him on his forehead. Startled he woke up with a sudden jolt.

"Hi mom, Max." "Have you seen the baby yet?"

"Not yet," Colleen answered. "We first wanted to check on Jenna?"
"How is she doing?" "What do the doctors say?"

Eric could hear the genuine concern in his mother's voice. He told them the doctor's said I could wake up at any time. He would just have to be patient because I had sustained a pretty bad blow to the head. Eric hugged his mother tightly and told her how much it meant to him that she was here. Eric told his mother and Max to go see their new granddaughter and spend as much time with her as they wanted. Colleen and Max returned to my room an hour later. She told Eric how beautiful our daughter was and she had her daddy's black hair and blue eyes.

A few days later Olivia was released from the hospital and Colleen offered to take care of our daughter until I was well and back home. After being in a coma for eight days I awoke with Eric asleep in a chair next to my bedside. His shirt hung out of his pants and his hair looked like it hadn't been combed in days. I reached over and touched his hand. My touch startled him as he turned towards me with a sweet smile on his face. The look on his worried face told me just how distressed he was. The first thing he told me was that he loved me and that our daughter was fine and was already dismissed and back home safe and sound in the most trusting care. By the end of the week, I was dismissed and, on my way, back home to my beautiful baby girl and I couldn't wait for her to be in my loving arms.

As Eric opened the front door, I heard a woman's voice singing and talking to Olivia. Even though the voice sounded familiar I just couldn't place it. As I entered the kitchen, I was blown away to find Colleen standing and holding our daughter. She was gently planting kisses on her face. Upon seeing me see put Olivia back in her high chair and walked over to me and wrapped her arms around me and placed her face into the side of my neck. I could feel her tears.

"Jenna, I've been such a stubborn jackass." "Please forgive me."

"I was just so upset with you and I was wrong." "You are my best friend and I am so ashamed of the way I treated you."

I wrapped my arms tightly around my best friend and told her as hurt as I was, I could understand and forgive her. I wanted her to know how much I loved Eric and I very much wanted her to be a part of our family. Colleen and I continued to talk as tears rolled down our faces. I finally had my best friend back.

Colleen stayed with us for another week helping me with Olivia. Once she had returned to Miami, we were back to calling each other a few times a week. It was as if our lives hadn't skipped a beat.

Eric and I remained in Santa Monica but sold the condo and bought a beautiful house with a magnificent view of the Pacific Ocean. I, in turn, sold my house in Miami to Linda, Professor Williams' daughter. Her family fell in love with the house while I lived in California. I was glad I was able to sell it to a lovely family.

****

Sometimes when Olivia is down for her nap, I find myself staring into her crib looking at her sweet angelic face and wonder what life would have been like with Ethan. I can't let my mind drift there. I was fortunate to have been loved by two wonderful men who loved me with every breath they had and have. I am blessed with a beautiful daughter and for her, I must look forward and never back. I loved Ethan, his love seemed like a lifetime ago, but with Eric, it's completely different and special. When he confessed to loving me since he was younger, I could not understand how he remained steadfast and committed to me. I knew it took a special person

and that was Eric, the man I would always love
and cherish.

I've often reflected back on my life. A life not
protected by the safety bubble that I never lived
in. I think life has a way of changing and challeng-
ing you for the better. Some people may not
agree with my philosophy, but it definitely
shaped and molded me into the strong and resili-
ent woman I am today.

My Angel

Do I dare ask who you are?
Do I dare ask where you came from?
You are like the moon shining in the evening sky
You are like the bright sun in the heavenly sky
Do I dare ask where you came from?

Sometimes you are like the falling raindrops
That drenches me in your love
Sometimes you are like the
sound of a bird's beautiful song
That wakes me in the morning
Do I dare ask where you came from?

Sometimes you are like the beautiful rhyme of a
poem
That contains the beauty of the entire universe
Sometimes you are like a gentle breeze
That makes my day brighter
Do I dare ask where you came from?

Sometimes you are like a child shedding tears
That desires just to be loved
Sometimes you are like a fortress
That is ready to protect
Do I dare ask who you are?

Junaid Majeed

Acknowledgements

Special thanks to the following people for their support, guidance and inspiration in the making of this book.

To Nella Guilarte for her fantastic cover illustration. To Montez Mack for putting everything together so that I could publish this novel. To my best friend Martha Camus, for always being there for me and always being my inspiration for the character of being my main characters confidant.
Special thanks to Junaid Majeed for contributing his beautiful love poem.

www.ingramcontent.com/pod-product-compliance
Lightning Source LLC
Chambersburg PA
CBHW071539150726
48000CB00002B/871